WAKEFIELD CRIME CLASSICS

DEATH IN DREAM TIME

Sidney Hobson Courtier was born in Kangaroo Flat, Victoria, in 1904 and died in 1974. He published twenty-six crime novels after the second world war, including many featuring 'Digger' Haig, the hero of *Death in Dream Time*. Courtier's fiction reflects his love of the Australian bush and fascination with puzzles, clues and ciphers.

Death in Dream Time was first published in London in 1959, and has not been published in Australia before its release in Wakefield Crime Classics, the series that revives forgotten or neglected gems of Australian crime and mystery fiction.

Also available in

WAKEFIELD CRIME CLASSICS

THE WHISPERING WALL
by Patricia Carlon

THE MISPLACED CORPSE
by A.E. Martin

BEAT NOT THE BONES
by Charlotte Jay

LIGNY'S LAKE
by S.H. Courtier

SINNERS NEVER DIE
by A.E. Martin

A HANK OF HAIR
by Charlotte Jay

THE SECRET OF THE GARDEN
by Arthur Gask

VANISHING POINT
by Pat Flower

THE SOUVENIR
by Patricia Carlon

DEATH IN DREAMTIME

S. H. COURTIER

Series editors Michael J. Tolley and Peter Moss

Wakefield Press
Box 2266
Kent Town
South Australia 5071

First published in 1959
Published in Wakefield Crime Classics in July 1993

Copyright © The estate of S.H. Courtier, 1974
Afterword copyright © Michael J. Tolley and Peter Moss, 1993

All rights reserved. This book is copyright. Apart from any fair
dealing for the purposes of private study, research, criticism or
review, as permitted under the Copyright Act, no part may be
reproduced without written permission. Enquiries should be
addressed to the publisher.

Edited by Jane Arms
Designed by Design Bite, Melbourne
Printed and bound by Hyde Park Press, Adelaide

Cataloguing-in-publication data
Courtier, Sidney Hobson (1904-1974)
Death in Dream Time
ISBN 1 86254 295 3
I. Title. (series: Wakefield Crime Classics)
A823.3

CHAPTER 1

Jock Corless crossed from New South Wales to Queensland by Benogra at 9.35 one warm, wet Tuesday morning.

A motel is strategically situated on the Queensland side of the border gate, and there Corless paused for petrol, directions and a quick meal, thereby unconsciously awarding himself the accolade of luck. Some hours later, when the Winonga police telephoned through, the owner of the border establishment was not only able to recall the time of Corless's brief stay and name the make of his car but also describe him in some detail.

'Big fellow,' the motel proprietor told the official voice at the other end of the line. 'Six foot one and thirteen and a half stone. Dark hair, grey eyes, tough jaw. About twenty-seven years. Looks like a fighter but nice enough to talk to. Driving a steel-grey Goddess. What's he been up to?'

The official voice ignored the question and coldly inquired, 'What time did he leave you?'

'Ten o'clock on the dot. Watched him go. The Goddess took off like a bird. Remember wishing I could afford a car – '

But the owner of the official voice, not interested in a motelier's aspirations, ended the conversation.

Meanwhile Corless, who looked like a fighter but was simply a sedate storekeeper from the Riverina town of Lake View, travelled through the warm rain in his Goddess at a steady fifty-five. At a quarter to twelve, edging round a shoulder of Creeping Hill – the rain had eased slightly but a fog had settled in – he saw a large sign that marked a junction:

UNGAMILLIA, DREAM TIME LAND
Two miles of Steep Winding Road

He ignored this junction. Another half mile of the twisting highway brought him to a second sign which read, 'The Well of St Giles, 300 yards', and he had a cold, goose-fleshy feeling at the thought of what his cousin, Laurie Moore, might have to tell him.

Laurie was at the Well, but Corless did not see him straightaway because of the crowd. A policeman in a slouch hat and a dripping cape waved the Goddess in behind a line of halted vehicles.

'There's been an accident,' he explained. 'I'm afraid you'll have to wait till we get things cleared up.'

'I suppose I can have a look,' Corless said, thinking that the accident need not interfere with his meeting with Laurie.

'As long as you don't get in the way,' warned the policeman.

Corless climbed out on to the greasy bitumen, donned a raincoat and set off past the immobilised traffic. The rain slid down quietly. Patches of fog rose from a gorge-like valley on the left; more fog drifted sluggishly through the tall trees on Creeping Hill. The scene was dank and dismal and so were the people at the Well.

Cars travelling in the opposite direction had also been halted. Between the two lines of vehicles was a gap of about forty yards occupying the arc biting into the hill where the Well was placed. Corless could see the stone wall of the Well and the conduit carrying water to it from a spring high up in the embankment. A solitary car waited in this gap, and a policeman and several civilians stood round a singularly distraught man. Another policeman measured skid marks that had obviously been left by the solitary car. Behind the car a police sergeant and two other men knelt by someone who lay supine on the ground. A score or so of people stood on the edge of the road with their backs to the valley. One of them, a girl, was weeping and an earnest young constable endeavoured to comfort her.

Corless did not see Laurie in any of the groups. He moved around quietly. No one took particular notice of him. He listened to the distraught man for a while, gradually making sense of his story. He had been coming up from Winonga, making over the hills towards the coast and driving slowly because of the rain and fog. He was just rounding the curve at the Well when something flashed down the embankment and dropped right in front of the radiator.

'I hit it with a bump,' he said, his lower lip twitching. 'I thought it was a wallaby. Damn things are always jumping in front of cars. I stopped to see if it had done any damage and I looked back – *and it was a man!* I hadn't a chance, I tell you. I couldn't help hitting him. I didn't see him till he jumped right in front of me. And that's God's truth – '

The fog seemed to get into Corless's throat then. He joined the group round the supine man. The sergeant glanced up at him, but he did not speak. Corless could not have answered if he had, for the man on the ground was Laurie. There was a horrible wound in his head. Blood, softening and dispersing under the rain, had gushed from his mouth and nose. You did not have to look twice to see that he was dead.

It could have been Jack Corless lying there and not Laurie Moore, for there had been a close likeness between the cousins. But no one could have picked the likeness then – not with Laurie's face battered out of shape and covered with blood. Without reasoning why, Corless pulled his coat collar up round his chin.

The sergeant spoke to one of the men. 'It was lucky you happened along then, doctor, but you can't do anything. I wish that ambulance would come.' He straightened up and looked round and his voice rose. 'Bailey, I want you.'

He lumbered away, his boots squelching, and the earnest

young policeman who had been comforting the weeping girl tailed self-consciously after him.

Corless became aware of a man sitting on the coping-stone of the Well. He was large and lean, he wore an old water-soaked raincoat and he watched Corless with dark, sardonic eyes. Behind him, the clay was pallid red and wet like newly bled flesh. Above him were tall trees and jungle-thick scrub. Corless forgot the saturnine man. If the driver of the fatal car was right, Laurie had jumped from that damp covert just in time to be killed.

Or had fallen. Or had been pushed.

He should have spoken to the police then, should have said, 'Look, I'm this man's cousin. I've just driven six hundred miles to meet him here at the Well of St Giles right now at midday. He was in trouble. He wanted my help. You go on from there.'

But he said nothing at all. He had a deep, unformed feeling of something sinister. He wanted to think it out, and he couldn't think clearly with all these people gaping, the rain streaming down and Laurie lying in front of him, dead.

Retreating cautiously, he made himself an inconspicuous member of the larger group on the edge of the road. The girl, her tears dried now, was talking to the police sergeant. Corless judged her to be twenty-three or four. She wore a belted transparent plastic raincoat that invested her trim figure with long graceful lines. Her eyes were a deep blue-purple. Her hair was dark with mahogany-red lights gleaming in the curls.

'The point is this,' the sergeant was telling her, and Corless's ears pricked. 'We were on our way to Ungamillia to talk to Moore. That's how we were on the spot so quickly. We were only a minute behind the car that hit him and you were just behind us.'

The girl said, 'Five of you coming out to talk to Laurie!'

Corless could see only four policemen. The earnest Constable Bailey was now assisting in the measuring of skid marks.

The sergeant reddened. 'He's caused us some trouble at other times.'

Again it was Corless's cue to declare himself, but he did not and immediately had a kind of reward, for the sergeant went on, 'Now, Miss Flax, I understand you and Mr Mallet were in Winonga this morning, which is how *you* came to be on the scene – '

Julie Flax! £21. 13. 1d! And the thickest man with the bitter face beside her was Ovid Mallet. £1,118. 9. 1d was *his* share. He was big time.

The rain still trickled down, the fog continued to wreathe the trees. Round the bend came an ambulance feeling its way past the cars. It stopped at the Well, two men got out and took a stretcher from the rear. They lifted Laurie on to the stretcher, covered him with a blanket and slid him into the ambulance. They conferred briefly with the sergeant and the doctor, then the vehicle reversed delicately and set off back to Winonga.

The show was over. The road block was lifted. Corless returned to the Goddess, sat behind the wheel and waited. He watched the cars go by. Presently came a big car driven by Julie Flax. Beside her was Ovid Mallet, talking urgently, his sallow face seeming all nose and sour lips. They passed without looking at Corless.

Finally he set his own car moving. He drove slowly towards the Well, and wheeled round to return the way he had come. The Well of St Giles was deserted, only some dark stains rapidly disintegrating under the rain remaining to mark where Laurie had died.

Then he realised the place was not deserted. Just as he turned the corner, he caught a glimpse in the rear vision mirror of a man scrambling up the muddy embankment. In that short look, he recognised the dark-visaged man in the sodden raincoat who had been sitting on the coping stone. He was on the point of stopping, then he remembered that Julie had spoken of *five* policemen. Perhaps this man with the ugly face was the fifth, in which case it would be wise to keep on going.

Where the large sign fronted the highway, he took the steep side-road that led left to Ungamillia, home of Dream Time Land. He followed the glistening ribbon of bitumen coiling up through the gloomy jungle and thought of his cousin. Laurie was dead, but he felt no particular grief, only dismay and horror. They had never been close even as children, for Laurie was the senior by several years and, when Corless was old enough to come to terms with him, he had broken away from home to follow his own wilful career. His mother, who had brought Corless up, had died a few months before; died, Corless thought, with pain in her heart for her wayward son.

Laurie had written home at the time, but he had not come to the funeral. Maybe he'd had a satisfactory reason for staying away, but Corless would not have accepted it. Only the then apparently insignificant fact that he was working for Austin Flax, the old bushman who had established his Dream Time Land on the top of Creeping Hill, had emerged from that letter.

Corless thought that the Winonga police no doubt had good reason for wanting to interview Laurie. Yet he had called for help. And now he was dead. Maybe his six creditors could offer an explanation.

The Goddess arrived at another fork in the road. One arm swept up to the left climbing through an uninviting cutting; the other turned more gently to the right and curled round the hillside. Left to himself, Corless would have chosen to go right, but in the middle of the junction was a wobbly sign marked 'Ungamillia', and it pointed left. So that was the way he went.

Five minutes later, he was prepared to swear somebody had made a gross mistake with that sign. The cutting flattened into a narrow ledge hacked out of the hill, the bitumen gave place to gravel and the gravel yielded to clay so slippery that his wheels spun dangerously as they bit into the savage slope. He drove on grimly. His only comfort was that, if he did slide off the track, he could not go far. On the right was the embankment, on the left a wall of subtropical jungle; trees, ferns, creepers, stunted palms, fallen logs, woven together in an impassable mass.

He damned the sign. The rain had ceased, but he had climbed right up into the cloud. The trees were weird etchings on a dank canvas of fog. Jays called from somewhere above him, their harsh yacketing muted yet dragging down the hill as though the trees were pillars of vast echoing vaults.

Then he discovered he was getting somewhere. Above the embankment appeared a tall fence marching straight through the jungle; a peculiar double fence consisting of two ten foot walls of wire mesh, stretched tautly, with the tops of three foot space between them protected by drum-tight strands of barbed wire and more barbed wire making an overhang on the outer side.

It was obvious that unauthorised entry into Dream Time Land was discouraged.

The fence turned right and with it went the track, and then the track bent right again and ended at a big strong gate that bore the name 'Ungamillia'. Corless pulled the handbrake on hard, got out and chocked one of the rear wheels with a large stone, after which he studied the gate. It was locked from the inside, but, strangely, a small wicket in the middle of the gate was unlocked. He pushed this open and stepped through on to a gravelled drive that angled to the left under masses of overhanging foliage.

The clouds seemed to be lifting, but when he walked round a bend the jungle canopy shut gloomily down on him. In the gloom were two naked myalls with spears levelled head high.

Corless did a violent back-leap. Then he laughed shakily. This was the kind of thing you should expect to see in Dream Time Land. The warriors were merely dummies. He went on, laughing at himself again, but he was still shaken.

He entered a large glade or plat where on the right the vines were so thick and regular there was reason to think they had been deliberately trained that way. On the other side, he saw the fence again, but its character had changed. It was now a single fence, no more than four feet high, of close-set galvanised-iron posts and heavy wire mesh.

The reason for the change was obvious. There was no need for a double barrier on the edge of a precipice. Corless peered over at the matted tops of trees forty feet below. A dead tree trunk rose through the leaves and climaxed in a broken spire fully twenty-five feet above the level of the glade. It was a gigantic tree. He judged it to be ten feet in diameter at the top. He wondered how tall it had been when it was alive.

He turned to go on. He heard the jays calling again, the echoing effect now more pronounced, an indication that the cloud was really lifting. But the jungle remained wet and dark so that the black face peering out from the mat of creepers on the right looked ominously alive.

Prepared this time, he grinned, winked at the face and walked on without pausing. The black eyes seemed to follow him. He reached a turn in the drive, was about to head round it when a sudden impulse drove him back to take a second look at the face.

His heart gave an almighty throb. The face had gone.

He stood painfully still and stared at the tangle of vine. The jays were silent now, but small rustling noises came out of the jungle as though the dark growth concealed secret paths along which crept malignant watchers.

He was running before he knew what he was doing. He pulled himself down to a walk and swore angrily. The disappearing black face was part of the eerie Aboriginal programme Dream Time Land provided for its visitors. Only a fool would let his nerves play tricks here.

No more than thirty seconds later, all his resolution was ripped to shreds. A diabolical scream burst from somewhere above him and went racketing and echoing round the hill.

CHAPTER 2

The scream was repeated twice, an inhuman noise that wrecked all composure. Before Corless could move, someone spoke demoniacally. 'Damn you, Austin Flax!'

'And damn you, too!' cried another voice.

There was a sudden crashing and trampling and a little old man in wet clothes forced his way through the undergrowth and jumped out on to the drive.

'Did you,' he said, shaking a gnarled brown fist at Corless, 'see Genghiz Khan?'

Corless gulped down his astonishment. 'See *who?*'

'Genghiz Khan!' the old man barked impatiently. His open waistcoat hanging damply over a faded blue shirt quivered with his irritation.

'Who or what is Genghis Khan?' asked Corless.

'A blasted great big white cockatoo,' snapped the old man. 'Now don't stand there an' say you didn't see him. I heard him meself just a minute ago.'

Light dawned on Corless. He silently repeated his self-castigation, though it must be allowed that if you were not ready for it a cockatoo's scream could be demoralising.

He looked at the old man and said, 'Are you Mr Austin Flax?'

The old fellow's blue eyes blazed. 'Don't call me *mister!* I'm Austin Flax. *Mister* – hell! Only crawlers tryin' to bilk me call me that. Where's this damned Genghiz Khan?'

'I didn't see him, I only heard him,' replied Corless.

'I got to get him before he ruins everythin',' said Austin Flax, and he dived at the timber opposite to where he had emerged.

Just as abruptly he turned and came back and, hooking a finger under Corless's lapel, whispered conspiratorially, 'Boy, you be careful. Y're in Dream Time Land where you oughtn't to be. If I had Bucktooth Tommy here – but I ain't got him – If you spot anythin', come an' tell ol' Austin, now won't y'?'

For a moment, the fierce blue eyes lost their heat and showed only wistful appeal. He jerked round and went crashing through the undergrowth.

In the distance, Genghis Khan raised his cracked voice. 'Damn you, Austin Flax!'

'An' damn you, too!' said Austin Flax.

There, reflected Corless, goes £220. 11. 1d.

He became aware that someone else had arrived on the scene. A fair-haired, brown-eyed young man, dressed in plaid shirt and stained fawn trousers, smiled good-humouredly at him. At first glance a very pleasant young fellow.

The newcomer nodded. 'Quite a turn, isn't he?'

Corless said, 'He's unusual, anyway.'

The young man listened to the sounds of Austin Flax's progress through the jungle. 'But don't think he's a fool,' he said with sudden solemnity. 'Old Austin's anything but.'

'I haven't suggested anything of the kind,' said Corless.

The young man looked him up and down and said, 'I suppose you know you're trespassing. People usually pay a pound to get where you are now.'

'Blame the man who left the wicket gate open,' said Corless. 'And blame the sign that pointed left instead of right down at the junction. When I got to the gate, I walked in. I refuse to back down that track.' He took out his wallet. 'Here's your quid.'

'The sign points right,' said the young man.

'It didn't when I came along.'

The young man's eyes narrowed. 'Then somebody must have been monkeying with it. No. Put your money away. You'll be a guest of the house. You're Jock Corless, aren't you?'

'I am, and how did you know?'

'Poor Laurie used to talk about his cousin who runs a Lake View store, and you're pretty like Laurie.'

'What's your name?'

'Carl Rusking,' said the young man, putting out his hand.

'£22. 13. 1d,' said Corless to himself.

'Are you in charge here?' he asked, as they exchanged grips.

'You've got good judgment,' said Rusking. 'I am in charge. In fact, I'm Dream Time Land. I thought the idea up. I planned it, worked it out, made the models of the blacks. You've probably seen some of my work down there. But' – he proffered a cigarette case – 'don't tell Austin I said so. He likes to think he's the big wheel, and we let him. He does know his blacks. This is a rotten business about Laurie. It's knocked us all in a heap. All I can do is offer my sympathy.'

'Thanks,' said Corless. He took a cigarette and they lit up.

'It's damnable,' said Rusking. 'We can't work out how or why it happened. Somehow he got in front of that car and that's all we know. A foul business.'

There was something strange about this conversation and all at once Corless realised what it was. Rusking, who could have learnt of Laurie's death only in the last few minutes, spoke as though he assumed or knew that Corless did not have to be told about the fatality. Corless chose the second alternative. He had been seen and recognised down at the Well of St Giles.

'I was coming through this way on a trip to Brisbane,' he said. 'I thought I'd look Laurie up. It's been an unpleasant shock.'

Rusking's brown eyes slid at him. 'Did Laurie know you were coming?'

'No,' said Corless, pleased that he was literally telling the truth. 'And now – well, I suppose things have got to be talked over, his affairs, and so on. A funeral, for instance. Who's the best one to see? Austin Flax?'

Rusking shook his head. 'Not Austin. He's no fool, but he's occupied with his own matters. I guess Julie Flax is the one to see. She's Austin's daughter, by the way. She's the business head, and she and Laurie worked together on what you might call the box-office side of this show. She knows as much about his affairs as any of us.'

Corless remembered the girl weeping at the Well and wondered if there had been more than business relations between Laurie and Julie Flax.

'I'll have to get my car up from that gate first,' he said.

'I'll tell you what,' Rusking said. 'I've got the key of the big gate here. We're in a rush this afternoon with tourists coming so, to save time, you give me your car keys, and I'll go down and get the car, and you can go on up and see Julie. I've got to lock that wicket gate in any case.'

'That's very good of you,' said Corless, passing the keys over.

'No trouble. Just keep going up this drive and you'll come to the Dream Time main entrance. You'll see the house in front of you from there.' The brown eyes became thoughtful. 'But I don't quite follow how you got in. That small gate is never unlocked.'

'Well, I didn't bust it open,' said Corless. 'You'll see that for yourself. Maybe Laurie went that way to the Well and *he* left it open.'

Rusking nodded slowly. 'That could be it. Yes, I believe you've got it.' Then he gave Corless a jolt. 'Okay, I'll see you later. And don't worry about me handling your car. I've driven Goddesses.'

Wham! said Corless silently, then posed himself a question. Why should Rusking have to tell him he'd been recognised at the Well?

The gate, under a fantastic imitation of a *mia-mia* that bore the sign 'ALCHERA, THE DREAM TIME LAND', passed him on to the tonsure of Creeping Hill. The jungle on the crown had been shaved off and in its place were wide lawns, stands of bougainvillea, masses of hibiscus, a row of flame trees and a two-storeyed, green-roofed stone house facing west.

Studying the house from the south side, Corless could see outbuildings in its rear – laundry, workshop, garage, maybe – and farther over the green-tiled roofs of more buildings. But he could not tell what these were. He guessed the road he should have taken made its ingress on that side.

He chose a path leading to the front of the house. A tremendous panorama opened from the crest of the hill. The garden sloped gently for a hundred yards, then the ground tipped suddenly to a line of timber, after which it fell into a vast abyss. Beyond the treetops was nothing until the eye reached tiny patches far below of grass and fallow and swale and ridge stretching out to distant hills capped by level masses of cloud. A township nestled in the valley like a collection of ants eggs. Winonga, Corless guessed. He thought that Austin Flax, gazing out over this prospect, must feel a god-like exaltation.

He walked along a gravelled path towards the front portico, then he stopped in surprise. Someone had sunk a hole in the middle of one of the beautifully shaven lawns. The clay had been piled up neatly and nearby was a heap of turf that had evidently been removed before the digging started.

'That,' said a cloyingly rich voice, 'is Mr Flax's latest dream.'

He swung round. A plump little brunette of a woman, exuding an impression of pampered softness, reclined in an easy chair and watched him with half-closed eyes.

'Dream?'

The woman nodded.

'We all dream here,' she said, and there was a drugged quality in her throaty voice. 'This is *Alchera*, the place of dreaming.'

'What does Mr Flax dream about?' asked Corless.

'He dreams he's still in Northern Territory, or wherever it is they dig for gold.' The plump woman sighed as though she was yielding to an overpowering urge to sleep. 'This is his sixth hole in a fortnight. Perhaps he also dreams someone will fall in them, for he always puts them in the most perilous spot, though I must say he usually replaced the divots nicely when he's finished with them. I am Mrs Delia Ashwood. Who are you?'

£1,131. 9. 1d, Corless thought, eyeing the somnolent lady. Now he had only one more creditor to identify, the person with the disturbingly familiar name of Martha Rea.

'My name is Corless,' he said.

The dark eyes opened alertly.

'Goodness! Then you are looking for Julie.'

Corless agreed that was so.

'You'll find her inside.' The eyelids drooped and Mrs Ashwood sighed again. 'To dream and to dream and to live dreaming. To dream the elemental dream of waking to magical life. To dream in formless nothing of the world we shall build when we awake. The Alchera. Our Aborigines knew by instinct what we have rejected, Mr Corless. Chaos reduced to beautiful order in the magic of a dream.'

The lovely voice was slurred as if Mrs Ashwood talked in her sleep.

'Beautiful dreamer,' murmured Corless. 'Don't awaken to me.'

Mrs Ashwood stared at him. 'I beg your pardon!'

'I asked how to find Miss Flax.'

For a moment it seemed that Mrs Ashwood would debate the truth of this statement, but she gave up the struggle before it started. 'Ring the bell', she said, 'and go into the hall and someone will find Julie for you.'

She closed her eyes again. There was another long, gentle exhalation of breath. Mrs Ashwood had surrendered to dreaming.

Corless pondered the probability of Ungamillia being a receiving-house for crackpots. He mounted the steps, pressed the bell button and entered the hall. It was wide and spacious with a polished stairway leading to the upper floor, but it seemed overcrowded because of the bewildering display of Aboriginal weapons and implements cluttering walls and tables. Spears and nulla-nullas, woomeras and digging-sticks, death-bones and kurdaitcha shoes, head-dresses and pubic bands – Aboriginal war, peace and magic were all represented. Austin Flax, or someone, had an assiduous magpie instinct.

A door opened behind the staircase and a girl appeared. She had luminous grey eyes and silky brown hair and she wore a white dress that had something of the air of a uniform. She looked at Corless as though he were repulsive. 'What are you doing here?' she demanded.

Her voice was musical but it grated on Corless.

'Don't alarm yourself,' he said loftily. 'I'm not here because of you. I wouldn't have come if I'd known I'd meet you.'

Martha Rea's trilling laugh was entirely meretricious. 'Alarm? You flatter yourself. The great Jock Corless! Give him the universe and he'll show you how it should be run! Like his little store at Lake View. Everything just so. Dear, dear! Well, you're looking at one part of the universe Mr Corless can't run.'

'I'll be damned before I'd want to run a silly, puffheaded, irresponsible, glasshouse trinket!' he said raging. 'My God! What an idea!'

The pearl-grey eyes sniped at him. 'Your ideas mean nothing to me.' she said. 'Neither do you.'

It was as though the past seven months had not existed, he thought with hot exasperation; the fight went on as though there had been no break.

'Now you mention meanings', he said, 'all you mean to me is the £2,120. 1. 4d Laurie Moore owed you. Very interesting, especially the one and fourpence.'

She was aghast. 'Laurie! Oh, I – I'd forgotten he was your – your cousin. All I can say is I'm dreadfully sorry.' Then blood flooded into her face. 'What did you say? Laurie owed me two thousand – What was it?'

'£2,120. 1. 4d', he said, and he pursued his advantage. 'Quite a sum, eh? You must have been more successful with Laurie than you were with me.'

She stepped back as though he had struck her. He face was white now. 'How low can you get!' she said. Her small jaw hardened. 'For your information, Laurie Moore owed me nothing. Not a penny. But I can guess why you'd invent such a despicable lie. I know the way you think. I'll tell you just this. I'm here because I'm the nurse-companion to a sick woman. Her husband died some time ago, and she had a nervous breakdown. I came here with her. I met Laurie only casually, but it would seem his death has more real meaning for me than it has for you.'

'I tell you,' he fumed, 'Laurie wrote to me and said the money was owing and – '

He stopped, because Martha Rea had turned and was hurrying towards the stairs.

'All right,' he called after her stiff back. 'Will you be good enough to tell Miss Flax I'd like to talk to her?'

Julie Flax came down two minutes later, her floral dress swaying with her lithe, graceful movements. Her dark hair showed the reddish gleam he had noticed at the Well of St Giles. In the half light of the hall, her eyes were more purple than blue, tiny, blue-white crescents appearing under the irises as she studied him gravely.

She offered a small, firm, sun-tanned hand, her grip surprising him with its strength. She used a delicately exotic perfume. He knew enough to understand you bought that kind of perfume at a fiendish price per ounce.

'You're Jock Corless, Laurie's cousin,' she said. He thought her voice was nicely balanced, not too light and not too throaty. 'I'm dreadfully sorry to meet you like this.'

She was calm and restrained, but Corless remembered that she had wept at the Well.

She opened the door into a large lounge to the left of the hall. It was a room with panoramic windows, and its ornaments continued the hall's Aboriginal motif. She took him to a window niche on the north side. From here he discovered there were more buildings on Creeping Hill than he had suspected. He saw a cafe, a row of motel-like cabins and a cluster of carports. Cars were parked in front of the cafe and groups of people wandered round the garden.

'The tourist season,' Julie said, with a brief smile. 'Thank goodness the rain has stopped. The people are here for the lorikeets and Dream Time Land.'

'Lorikeets?'

'They come twice a day to feed on the flame-trees, and they're cute. But you're not interested in that. You're here because of' – Julie caught her breath – 'because of Laurie.'

Corless said, 'You understand, Miss Flax, there'll be all sorts of questions and complications.'

'Call me Julie,' she said. 'Yes, I know there'll be complications. But we're still in a state of shock. I can't realise he's gone even though I saw him down there. I can't understand it. None of us knows why he was there, or what he was doing there.' The purple eyes opened at Corless. 'You were there, too.'

He nodded.

'Yes,' Julie said. 'Ovid said he saw you, said you must be Jock Corless. You're so like Laurie. Why didn't you speak to us there?'

He had been expecting this and had his answer ready.

'I arrived after Laurie – after the accident. A policeman pulled me up. When I discovered it was Laurie who was dead, it was such a shock I couldn't talk to anybody. I had to pull myself together.'

'You're a long way from home, Jock,' she said, watching him. 'You run a country store at Lake View, six hundred miles south.'

He caught her drift and said, 'I'm on my way to Brisbane on a business trip, and I thought I'd look Laurie up going through. It meant only another hundred miles and I hadn't seen him for some years.'

'He didn't expect you?'

'No,' Corless said, and then he wondered why she eyed him so strangely.

'You weren't very good friends, were you, Jock?'

Corless's mouth tightened. 'No. But I had a letter from him recently and he was in my mind. And now, well, when the police have finished with him, the usual dispositions will have to be made.'

She understood, and for a while they discussed morticians and funeral arrangements. But she still had that wary questioning in her eyes, and he suddenly realised why. To get to the Well of St Giles, he *had gone past* the large unmistakable sign indicting the turn-off to Ungamillia. If he had merely been be calling on Laurie while passing through he must have taken the Ungamillia road. Therefore his presence at the Well would, in the light of his story, be queer and suspicious.

He had a moment of uneasy qualms but, determining to ignore questions until they were asked, he guided the conversation back to Laurie himself. He learned that Laurie had been something more than Julie's assistant on the box-office side. In the few months he lived at Ungamillia, Laurie had developed into an indispensable handyman about the place. Everybody liked him, especially old Austin Flax and, as far as Julie knew, Laurie had reciprocated their regard.

'But,' she went on, 'he was, well – you're his cousin. You knew him. He was – '

She hesitated and Corless said, 'He was unstable.'

That's the word, I suppose,' she said reluctantly. 'He had to break out every now and then. He'd go down into Winonga and, well, I suppose you can guess.'

Corless nodded grimly. 'I know. He'd give the beer a wallop, want to fight everybody on sight and finish up in the cooler.'

'The last time it happened, it took five policeman to handle him,' Julie said. 'Old Austin thought he was wonderful. My father's always talking about what a hellraising young devil he was, and he said Laurie reminded him of his young days in the Territory. But Laurie wasn't bad. He was just wild. He loved fighting, but he never did any real harm. You look as though' – the cool watchfulness still in her eyes – 'you'd be the same yourself.'

'God forbid,' said Corless, that orderly trader whose delight was in the harmonious display and sale of goods and the regular succession of ledger entries, none of them red. But he wished he could rid her eyes of the suspicion. 'Julie,' he said, leaning forward, and so was again aware of her perfume. 'Is it possible Laurie got into an intolerable mess and decided – let's be frank – there was only one way out?'

'You mean he deliberately threw himself in front of that car? But why should he do that?'

'That's what I'm wondering,' said Corless, not missing a flicker of her expression. He thought she look frightened now. 'I told you he wrote me a letter. In it was a list of people he owed money to. Six amounts and some of them are huge. The largest is £2,120. 1. 4d, the smallest £21. 12. 1d. Your name is against the £21. 13. 1d.'

'You're joking.'

'No, I'm not. I assure you that.'

'Then Laurie must have been joking,' she said in a wondering tone. 'As if I count my money in odd pennies! He never owed me any money, Jock. He never owed money to anybody in Ungamillia.'

Another creditor repudiating a debt, thought Corless. What the devil had Laurie been up to?

Julie moistened her lower lip.

'Who else – ' she began and stopped. Corless knew she wanted to find out whose were the other names on Laurie's list. It was just as well she refrained from the question because he would not have told her. Not until he had first questioned the other creditors.

She looked at her watch and discovered the time to be ten past one. At two o'clock the lorikeets would fly in; at two-thirty the first part of Dream Time Journey was due to begin, and there was considerable preparation to be made. She and Corless would talk again; she wanted this matter of the alleged debts clarified. Meanwhile, he must be hungry; if he cared to join the party in the dining-room, she would get him something to eat.

Thinking of Martha Rea glowering at him, Corless refused politely and said he would go to the cafe. Julie tried to dissuade him, but he felt she was secretly relieved at his refusal.

She accompanied him into the hall and put her hand on his arm. 'You *are* like Laurie', she said. Then she added softly, 'We'll talk again, Jock.'

She turned back to the door behind the stairs, waving to him as she went through. He wondered what it was he had said that dissolved the suspicion from her eyes. But he was glad it was gone. He thought it would be very pleasant being liked by Julie Flax.

CHAPTER 3

Had Mrs Ashwood, that enthusiastic dreamer, still been on the portico, he would have asked *her* about the sum Laurie had put against her name. £1,131. 9. 1d it was. He knew them all off by heart now, for they had plagued his thoughts for days.

But Mrs Ashwood had taken herself away, presumably to lunch. The clouds had lifted, shrunken into woolly fluffs, and the sun patched the wide view with dark blues and pale, clear greens. On the north side rose the talk and laughter of many people. There was the sound of more cars arriving. It was obvious that, at a pound a head, Dream Time Land was a lucrative business.

Austin Flax marched round a corner, waistcoat flapping, boots crunching on the gravel, a shovel under one arm, on his shoulder a huge white cockatoo, whose bright black eye seemed as malignant as its curved beak. From Austin's lips emanated a noise that Corless managed to recognise as a weird version of 'Onward Christian Soldiers'.

The old man saw Corless and the cacophony ceased.

'I got him,' he said, rubbing his head against the cockatoo. 'Just as well, too. He's a mischievous animal.'

Genghiz Khan displayed his yellow crest and said, 'Damn you, Austin Flax.'

'An' damn you, too', retorted the old man genially. His fierce blue eyes probed at Corless. 'Well, young feller, spot anythin'?'

'I don't understand – ' began Corless.

Austin cut him off.

'Course you understand. I know who you are. Laurie's cousin, that's who. There was a boy. God knows, I'm goin' to miss him.'

'Mr Flax,' Corless said, 'did Laurie owe – '

'Don't call me mister!' the old man shouted angrily. 'Only illegitimate frogs' spawn call me mister. Me name's Austin Flax. Me black boy back in the Territory, Bucktooth Tommy, he'd be sick for a week if anybody called me mister. All a bushman wants is his name.'

'Okay, Austin. I want to know if Laurie owed you any money.'

'Owed me money!'

'To be exact, £222. 11. 1d.'

'Hell!' snarled Austin. 'He never owed me nothin'. He didn't have to. Anythin' I had was his. I liked that boy. He was a buckeroo.'

He stopped, peered upward and his manner altered. Corless looked up, too, and saw Mrs Ashwood languidly watching from a balcony in front of a top-storeyed window.

'Dreams,' growled the old man softly. 'I'd give her dreams. What she wants is a man to belt the daylights out of her.' With a complete change of tone he raised his voice. 'Well, boy, got to fill her in. Struck a duffer again. But I tell you there's gold in this 'ere hill. It's like Mount Morgan – all gold underneath, an' I'll find it. But this one missed.'

He stepped on to the lawn, put Genghiz Khan down, fastened a chain round the bird's leg, pegged the other end of the chain to the turf, then, seizing the shovel, began to fill the hole in expertly.

'Damn you, Austin Flax,' said Genghiz Khan, biting at the chain.

'An' damn you, too', said Austin Flax.

Corless went down through the garden, past groups of visitors chattering on the lawns, and entered the cafe. He found a vacant table near a window which gave him a view of the flame trees. The masses of brilliant scarlet blossom were a gorgeous fire against the sombre background of the jungle trees.

He was still gazing at them when a neat, dark-eyed waitress in a white uniform with blue facings approached.

'That's where the 'keets come,' she said. 'They're a wonderful sight in the flame trees, thousands of them, all green and gold. People come hundreds of miles to see them.'

'There's a big crowd here today,' said Corless.

'Nothing to the crowds we have had,' the girl said. 'The rain's stopped a lot. What would you like, sir?'

As Corless studied the menu, the girl spoke again. 'You're Laurie Moore's cousin, aren't you?'

Corless looked up. 'Did you know Laurie?'

'He and I – we were friends,' she said, and it seemed to Corless that her eyes filled with tears.

He wondered how close the friendship had been. She seemed a nice youngster, not the flamboyant type Laurie had liked to racket around with.

'What's your name?' he said.

'Elsie Mannus.' She hesitated as though there was more she wanted to say. Then she became business-like. 'What's your order, Mr Corless?'

He wasn't hungry, and he asked for a pot of tea and some sandwiches, and the girl went away. She had scarcely gone when a tall fair-haired young man occupied the spare chair, smiled across at Corless and said, 'Remember me?'

'Of course,' said Corless. 'What about my car?'

Rusking grinned and held out a bunch of keys. 'The Goddess is in one of the carports, and your bags are up in the house.'

Corless raised his eyebrows. Putting the keys away, he said, 'The bags in the house! Why?'

'Julie's orders. You'll be staying here. That is, I guess, till arrangements for poor Laurie are made.'

'But – '

Rusking waved away any possible objections. 'Couldn't be otherwise, Jock. You're Laurie's cousin, and this was his home. And you don't have to see Martha all the time.'

'What the devil!' said Corless, his face hot.

Rusking grinned. 'A word of advice, Jock. In this place, if you want to keep a secret, you write it in invisible ink on a piece of paper, go out into the bush, burn the paper carefully and let the wind blow the ashes away. The safest bet, of course, is to have no secrets at all.'

The waitress returned with Corless's tea and sandwiches.

Rusking said, 'Just a cup of tea for me, Elsie. I'm in a hurry. And tear Mr Corless's cheque up. He's the guest of Ungamillia.'

The girl retreated and Corless said, 'Thank you.'

Rusking brushed the thanks aside. 'I hear you've been asking about money matters,' he said pleasantly. 'Anything to ask me?'

Corless picked up a sandwich. 'Yes. According to a letter from Laurie, he owed you £212. 13. 1d. Correct?'

Rusking laughed. 'I'm one of the lesser creditors from what I hear. No, Jock, it's not correct, though if you insist, I won't refuse two hundred pounds. We won't fight over the odd figures. But, seriously, Laurie owed money to nobody here.'

'Then why on earth say he did?'

Rusking's brown eyes were suddenly sharp. 'Perhaps to make sure you came here. You wouldn't have come otherwise, would you?'

'I don't suppose I would have,' Corless said.

The waitress was back with Rusking's tea. He waited until she had gone before he continued. 'On the other hand, Jock, Laurie could have been joking. He was that kind of doer, you know.'

Laurie's letter, nestling in Corless's inner pocket, was sufficient evidence that whatever had been in his mind was not a joke.

They ate in silence for a while, then Rusking said, 'I guess the coroner will find it accidental death. That's the only verdict he can come to, though what Laurie was clambering above the road for God only knows.'

'No chance of suicide?'

Rusking said, 'Jock, your cousin got too much fun out of life even to dream of suicide. Ask the Winonga police. Get *that* out of your mind. Now I've got to race. Lorikeets, you know, and blackfellows' games to follow in Dream Time Land though, heaven above, with this happening to Laurie, there's not going to be much pleasure today. By the way, this might be interesting.'

He hurried out of the cafe, and Corless picked up the programme he had dropped on the table.

UNGAMILLIA

(Aranda for 'Evening Star')

PRESENTS

DREAM TIME LAND

THE STORY OF THE ALCHERA

Three years ago, Carl Rusking, a young Melbourne water-colourist and sculptor, seeking outlet for his creative urge, went to Central Australia and met Austin Flax, owner of the Monnadea Cattle Station. Out of this meeting grew DREAM TIME LAND. Austin Flax, the cattleman, had lived a lifetime with the Aranda tribes and so developed a unique understanding of their language, ways, customs ceremonies and myths. He had long wished to present the true story of these inland tribesmen to the public. With the help of Carl Rusking, the artist, this desire has been consummated in DREAM TIME LAND.

By means of nine dioramas, the fundamental beliefs of the Aranda are presented in simple and striking dramatic form. The bushman guiding the artist and the artist illuminating the bushman have resulted in a show that is unequalled anywhere in the world.

In this grand undertaking, they were assisted and inspired by Julie Flax, Austin Flax's daughter, an artist in her own right and almost as fine an authority on the Australian Aborigine as her father.

There is a standing offer to refund the price of admission to anyone who can prove that DREAM TIME LAND falls short of expectations. Only one person has made such an attempt. He has since been returned to the institution from which he escaped.

Then there followed details of the programme.

> Alchera One ... Apma awakes
> Alchera Two ... Apma wins a wife
> Alchera Three ... Apma -

At this point, Corless was interrupted. Ovid Mallet placed himself in the chair vacated by Rusking. His nose was arrogant, his eyes hot and insolent.

'I'm Mallet,' he said abruptly. 'What is the amount alleged to be owing me by your late cousin?'

Corless emptied his second cup of tea. He took his time to light a cigarette, all the while eyeing the sour man opposite him. '£1,118. 9. 1d,' he said.

'For what is the money owing?' demanded Mallet. 'Services rendered, a loan, goods supplied, backing a bill, transfer of property or what?'

A bell rang. Of course, Corless thought, of course. This fellow was a scion of the great house of Mallet who for generations had been Sydney's biggest storekeepers. The Mallet Emporium had branches in every capital city and leading provincial town. 'Our Front Window is Australia. You Name It, We Have It.'

He examined Mallet with fresh interest. 'Laurie gave me no reason why the money was owing,' he said.

'Not even a hint?'

'No.'

Mallet stood up. He looked at Corless with a contempt he didn't bother to conceal.

'Your cousin owed me nothing.' he said. 'I'll tell you what I think. This list of alleged debts is all fabrication. The work of a dark imagination.' He paused for three seconds, then added, 'Yours. I'm ready to amplify my remarks any time you like.'

He started to walk away, but as he turned something slipped from his pocket and fluttered to the floor. Corless picked it up. He had time to realise it was a small photograph depicting two naked men, one black, the other white, standing in a bush glade against a massive dark background. Then it was snatched out of his hand.

'Mine,' Mallet spat.

He stared into Corless's eyes as though waiting. Corless did nothing. Mallet turned and went away, this time not with stately tread but, Corless thought, more like a rat scurrying to its hole.

Corless smoked a second cigarette. Uneasiness gnawed at him. Only one more of Laurie's alleged creditors remained to be questioned, but he was certain that Mrs Ashwood's answer would be that Laurie had owed her nothing. Why then had he sent this list of amounts owing? Was it chance that he was dead before he could explain its meaning?

And what scurvy trick brought Martha Rea to Ungamillia? He had thought he was finished with that old business, that he was forgetting that Martha Rea had ever existed. Damn and damn! he said to himself and drifted outside.

Tourists were gathering round the flame trees although the lorikeets were not due for another twenty minutes. But, avoiding the tourists, Corless headed for the main gates, the proper entrance to Ungamillia. The crooked sign was still troubling him. Judging by the way cars streamed into the grounds, the sign must have been rectified. Either that, or the visitors knew which road to take.

One vehicle, a utility, did not enter, however. The driver climbed out, pushed something into a box on one of the posts, blew a shrill whistle and, getting back into the utility, drove off. The mailman from Winonga had arrived.

Corless opened the box and took the mail out. He looked through the letters curiously, wondering if there were any for Laurie.

Miss Julie Flax, Miss Julie Flax, Mrs D. Ashwood, A. Flax, C. Rusking, Esq., Miss M. Rea –

'Thank you', said a voice insultingly, 'but I collect the mail.'

Mallet again. Corless's hackles began to rise. 'You move around, Mr Mallet', he said.

'Irrelevant, Corless. I'll have those letters – now!'

'I don't care for your tone,' said Corless.

'Are you going to give me those letters, Corless, or have I got to take them?'

Corless deliberately sorted through the bundle. 'There's one for you, Mallet. You may have – '

Mallet grabbed the letters and headed for the house, not at a run precisely, but at such a clip that Corless would have had to run to catch up to him.

Corless shrugged his shoulders, reserving the right to act appropriately with Mallet later on. Then he discovered that Mallet had not got all the letters. One was lying on the ground, apparently dropped during the recent exchange. Corless picked it up and examined the peculiar superscription. It was printed in large purple letters as though done with a child's printing-set and it read:

>Mrs Delia Ashwood
>c/o Miss Julie Flax
>Ungamillia, via Winonga, Queensland

Corless perceived that despite the elaborate address the cancelled stamp bore the Winonga postmark. He noticed another odd feature. He bent the letter so that the enclosure was pressed hard against the envelope. But this envelope was stout. No trace of any writing or shadow penetrated its opacity. Still, he was prepared to bet the enclosure was a small photograph or postcard. A coincidence, he thought.

He put the letter in his pocket, resolving to hand it to Mrs Ashwood at the first opportunity.

At ten minutes to two, a small procession came down from the house. In front marched Austin Flax, still in waistcoat and faded blue shirt and mud-stained trousers. With him was Julie, now wearing slacks. Behind them minced the dreamful Mrs Ashwood with Martha Rea beside her, cool and watchful. In the rear were Carl Rusking and Ovid Mallet. The pound a head audience became still, thereby enabling Corless to realise that Austin was again humming his version of 'Onward Christian Soldiers'.

Then Corless had a surprise. A lean, ugly visage suddenly stood out among the tourists. While everyone else looked at the procession, this face turned towards Corless, bunched ridges of hard flesh above the corners of the mouth conveying a predatory cynicism. Corless stared back into the dark eyes. The last time he had seen this man, he had been climbing the wet embankment behind the Well of St Giles. His hat was pulled down over one side of his displeasing countenance. His coat hung carelessly open. His tie was tucked inside his shirt. Every line of his face and figure shouted a tough disregard for what anybody thought.

The procession arrived. 'Onward Christian Soldiers' ceased. Mrs Ashwood and Martha Rea stayed with the audience, but Julie, Austin, Rusking and Mallet took up prominent positions in front of the flame trees.

The old man looked at his watch, had a few words with his companions and faced the crowd.

'Folks,' he began. 'Thank you for comin' to Ungamillia this afternoon, an' a hearty welcome to Dream Time Land. I'm sure you won't be disappointed at what an old bushman's got to show you.'

'Hear, hear!' said Rusking with a grin that made everybody grin with him; everybody that is, except Mallet, whose expression would have curdled desert sand.

'Now about these 'keets you're goin' to see,' continued Austin, his blue eyes good-humoured. 'They're well known in Queensland. In fact, they're common. But they're beautiful birds. They come here every mornin' at half past nine an' every afternoon at two o'clock as near as dammit.'

'Four minutes to two, Austin,' interposed Rusking smiling.

'Hell, boy, I can tell the time,' said the old man. 'About these gold necks. When they come they'll swarm all over the trees. They'll take no notice of you. All they want is the honey in the flowers. You can get as close as you like but don't touch 'em, because they'll bite. Just let 'em entertain you.

'I don't know why they arrive here dead on the tick twice a day. Far as I c'n see, the honey's just as sweet any other time. But that's what they do, an' they keep on doin' till the blossom season's over, then they go away an' don't come back till next season. Now, folks' – Austin looked at his watch – 'any moment now.'

The lorikeets made a liar out of Austin Flax. It was not until four minutes past two that they arrived. After a preliminary whirr and clatter down in the jungle, a scintillating green cloud arose and then the lorikeets descended, screeching upon the blossom.

The trees became a trembling mass of scarlet, green and gold. Every calyx had little curved beaks probing deep into it. As they explored the flowers, the lorikeets fluttered, hovered, swung upside down. They buffeted each other out of the way and fought furiously when two or three happened to invade the same blossom. There was an impression of intense, vivid, green vitality. The bright black eyes were like questing polished jewels, the slender little bodies a lovely green and gold iridescence. The air shivered with their screeching chatter.

The tourists broke ranks and crowded round the trees, some with cameras out recording the scene. The lorikeets were undismayed even when faces and cameras ventured within six inches of them. Children made as much noise as the birds. Austin Flax was the centre of an excited group all asking questions. He expanded magnificently under the attention.

Corless felt a touch on his elbow and turned to look into Mrs Ashwood's soft slumbrous face.

'A fine show, Mr Corless', she said, her beautiful voice making the words sing.

Corless agreed politely.

'A pity if it is spoiled.'

'I beg your pardon.'

'You've been asking questions,' said Mrs Ashwood. 'I'm going to ask one. What amount was your cousin supposed to owe me?'

'£1,131. 9. 1d.'

Mrs Ashwood said sadly, 'An impossible amount even if he did owe me money, which he didn't. I don't like this, Mr Corless. I'm here for rest and recuperation. It is a wonderful place. This scene is merely the introduction to a supreme experience. Don't ruin it, Mr Corless. And please no more disturbing my companion. Please!'

'I beg your pardon again!' said Corless, startled.

'I refer to my nurse-companion, Martha Rea. I haven't been well, and she is looking after me. Anything that disturbs her disturbs me. You will please leave her alone. I don't want her unhappy.'

Martha was about six paces away, apparently absorbed in watching the lorikeets.

Corless raised his voice somewhat. 'I won't disturb your companion, Mrs Ashwood. I wouldn't disturb her for anything in the world. I'd rather disturb a thousand bull-ants' nests. And, while I think of it, here's a letter for you. Mr Mallet left it behind when he collected the mail.'

He handed the letter over. He turned away with cool dignity. But his lofty carriage was shattered by an appalling screech that ripped through the noise of the lorikeets. He bounced round in time to see a large white cockatoo land plump in the middle flame tree. The next moment the lorikeets rose with a whirring of wings and fled panic-stricken for the jungle.

Genghiz Khan dropped to the ground and strutted, emitting proud chuckles.

Austin Flax gave an enraged bellow. 'Who let that blasted bird loose?'

He rushed at Genghiz Khan, who rose in the air and flew for the house with the old man in hot pursuit. As Genghiz Khan turned the corner, his raucous voice floated back.

'Damn you, Austin Flax!'

'An' damn you too!' Austin Flax shouted murderously. 'File that,' said a morose, gravelly voice in Corless's right ear, 'under Turns, Well-Rehearsed.'

The saturnine man stared at Corless with a bushranger glint in his dark eyes.

CHAPTER 4

'Ladies and gentlemen,' declaimed Rusking affably. 'We'll let Austin chase Genghiz Khan all over Asia – er – Ungamillia, and proceed to Dream Time Land. Austin will rejoin us there.'

With some good-humoured banter, the assemblage began to move across the garden to the artificial *mia-mia* giving entry to the Alchera.

'Yair,' said the ugly man. 'A stunt. But it gets 'em in.' His bent nose slanted at Corless. 'I want a word with you, young feller.'

'What about?'

'For a start, say all this money your late cousin is said to have owed.'

'Who is asking?'

A sinewy brown hand pulled a folder from a pocket. Inside the folder was a card that proclaimed that the bearer was Detective-Inspector C.J.Haig, CIB, Brisbane.

'File me under pleasant surprises,' said Inspector Haig. 'My friends call me Digger.'

'Why?'

'Shall we say I dig the facts out?'

'Why are you interested in my cousin?'

Eyeing Corless darkly, Haig said, 'Because he was dead before that car hit him at the Well of St Giles.'

Corless's forebodings congealed in a lump in his chest. He said, 'How do you know that?'

'The doctor in Winonga told me', said Haig. 'And I reckon a doctor ought to know.'

'How long before?'

'The doctor says no more than an hour.'

So it was murder!

The queue filed slowly through the *mia-mia* where Carl Rusking and Julie Flax worked busily at cash registers.

Corless said cheerfully, 'Brisbane is ninety miles from here. You are strangely on the scene.'

Haig's grin was malevolent.

'The same applies to you, Jock, only more so. The store you run at Lake View down in the Riverina is six hundred miles away.' The inspector studied the tourists moving through the gate. He said 'It'll be some time before the show opens. Time enough for you to explain the six hundred miles and the list of debts.'

'How do you know about that list?'

'If you want to keep a secret in this place,' Haig said, 'write it on a piece of paper in invisible ink, go out into the bush, burn the paper and let the wind blow the ashes away. I quote Mr Rusking. You and he sat near a window. Now come clean, Jock.'

They moved aside from the queue. Somewhere inside the jungle gloom of Dream Time Land rose a wavering, deep toned blare of queer variations in semi-tones that affected one like an electric vibration. Only the didgeridoo, the native hollow-log trumpet, could produce that galvanising noise.

The didgeridoo faded and wild voices began a chant:

> *Oknirra! Oknirra! Oknirra!*
> *Apma Oknirra!*
> *Wei! Wei! Wei!*

'Which, being interpreted,' said Inspector Haig, a gleam in his eye showing that even he felt the hot stimulation of the noise, 'means, "Great! Great! Great! The Snake is Great!

Three hearty cheers!" Regarding your cousin, Jock.'

Corless handed over Laurie's letter. Haig read silently, but Corless could follow easily for he knew that letter by heart. It had sent chills into his orderly trader's soul.

Dear Jock

If you tear this screed up and throw it in the fire, I won't be surprised. The fact is we have done nothing but ignore each other for years. It is also a fact that the fault is all mine.

How damned right you were, Corless always thought at this point.

I wish now it had been otherwise for I am in a hell of a mess and you're the only one I think might help me out.

Hell's holy bells! was Corless's reaction here.

I've got to see you. I can't explain everything in a letter. You wouldn't believe me and besides it wouldn't be safe. I can't go to you, so will you come to me? It's a lot to ask you to drive 600 miles, but I'll be waiting at St Giles' Well on Creeping Hill every day this week from midday to one o'clock. Please don't write, just come. A letter wouldn't get to me. And don't come to the house.

In case anything happens, I'm enclosing a statement of money owing. Study the amounts carefully.

Cheers, Jock. If all goes well, I'll try to make amends for things past.

Laurie

PS This is serious, Jock.

Haig held up the enclosed statement. 'Now that something's happened,' he said, 'I suppose you've studied these figures carefully.'

'I studied them carefully from the jump,' said Corless. 'I thought I was up for £4,824. 16. 9d.'

'Which would have been too bad', grunted Haig, and he

read the statement aloud.

> *Carl Rusking* ... £212. 13. 1
> *Mrs Ashwood* ... £1,131. 9. 1
> *Martha Rea* ... £2,120. 1. 4
> *Ovid Mallet* ... £1,118. 9. 1
> *Austin Flax* ... £220. 11. 1
> *Julie Flax* ... £21. 13. 1

'This,' said Haig, 'is queer.'

Corless had always realised its queerness. The odd shillings and pence, the similarities and repetitions. In a properly run business, odd shillings and pennies were a part of good bookkeeping, but Laurie had had no business. Money for him had been something you needed for a good time. The glorious science of bookkeeping had been beneath his contempt.

'The queerest thing,' said Haig, 'is that at least two creditors deny there was money owing.'

'They *all* deny it,' said Corless.

'Did you mention the amounts to them?'

'Of course.'

'Any reaction?'

'Apart from denying it, there was some scoffing at the shillings and pennies.'

'I should think so,' said Haig. 'To me, Jock, it's also queer that the largest amount should be against the girlfriend's name.'

Corless got hot under the collar. 'Martha Rea is not my girlfriend.'

'No?'

'No. I'll tell you this. There was a time when I would have married her. She was a hospital sister at Lake View and she nursed Laurie's mother – my aunt – through her last illness. We became very close. But the thing fell through, and she left Lake View, and I neither knew nor cared where she went. I had no idea she was here at Ungamillia and, when I saw her name on Laurie's list, I hoped it was someone else with the same name. I didn't come here because of her. And that's that,' Corless said, implying that he didn't want to hear any more of the unpleasant topic.

'I gather,' said Haig, 'you and your cousin weren't smothering each other with affection, so why *did* you come?'

Corless, still aware of the didgeridoo's throb and the harsh growl of native singing, thought back to the morning he had opened this letter.

'I came,' he said, 'because of four things Laurie wrote. The first was the comment, "A letter wouldn't get to me". The second, "In case anything happens". The third, his statement that he would try to make amends for things past, because – I'll speak frankly – he hurt his mother badly. She brought me up, and I had a lot of time for her. The fourth is the, "PS – This is serious, Jock."'

'And the debts?'

'If it had been just the money, I wouldn't have come.'

Haig said, 'Everybody here says there was no money owing. If they're right, then it's not a statement of debts at all.'

'In that case,' Corless said, 'what does it mean?'

'Maybe you could tell me.'

'Me! How could I tell you?'

'You could if you made it up,' said Haig. Then, as Corless flushed with anger, he held up his hand. 'Wait, Jock. You've got to explain two things. First, you were on the scene at St Giles' Well. You saw your dead cousin. Did you speak up and say, "Look, this is my cousin. I came here to meet him. God, what's happened?" No, Jock, you didn't. You snooped around, then drove off without saying a word.

'The second thing. You came into Ungamillia the back way as though you wanted to sneak in. Now what about it?'

Corless swallowed hard. 'I'll answer the second question first,' he said, and described his movements from the wobbly sign at the fork in the road to his meeting with Rusking, not omitting the vanishing black face and the encounter with Austin Flax.

Haig focused on the sign. 'When I came up less than an hour ago, the sign pointed the right way. Okay, Jock, don't argue. I only want your story. Now the first question.'

Finding his voice hard to control, Corless repeated what he had told Julie Flax: the shocking surprise of finding Laurie dead, the feeling he had to think it out before he spoke, that he had to find out more. And then there was something he had not told Julie: the impression, engendered perhaps by the rain the fog drifting through the jungle, by the mist smudging out the deep valley, that some grotesque evil had twisted Ungamillia into horror as a picture painted on a sheet of rubber becomes grotesque when the rubber is stretched.

'That's your story?' said Haig, the bushranger look back.

'Yes.'

'Okay. You don't have to prove it or disprove it. *I'll* do that.' The inspector's fingers fastened on Corless's elbow. 'Time we were moving in. The last of the line's through the gate. And because you're a wealthy storekeeper who can afford to run a Goddess and I'm only a poor policeman, you'll shout, Jock.'

Corless did shout. If Julie or Rusking had remained in the *mia-mia*, he and Haig, no doubt, would have been passed in. But Ovid Mallet was behind the grille. His face was stony as he accepted Corless's two pound notes.

Corless had taken ten paces towards the crowd now assembled near the first bend in the drive when he realised he was alone. He looked round. Haig was behind the *mia-mia*, talking to the Winonga sergeant of police and five or six constables, one of whom was the earnest young officer who had been so assiduous in comforting Julie at the Well of St Giles. Corless remembered that his name was Bailey.

Rusking climbed on a stump with his back pressed against a thick growth of clematis that cloaked the jungle.

'Ladies and gentlemen,' he said, and there was a change in him. Still pleasant, he was now deadly in earnest. 'You are in Alchera, the Land of the Dream Time. You are starting on what we may call the Dream Time Journey. In this journey, you will come to nine stations or, as we prefer to term them, nine Alchera, all arranged under the wise guidance of Austin Flax, who lived for many years among the myalls. These Alchera have been arranged for your entertainment and also, we hope, for your enlightenment. If you know what a blackfellow thinks and believes and why he thinks and believes these things, you will understand him. And that's what our blackfellows need today – understanding.'

Out of the ring of faces watching Rusking, Corless picked Martha Rea's cool features. Beside her was the exalted face of Mrs Ashwood.

'Now a word about the meaning of Alchera. This is the name given by Central Australian people to the time when the world was being made. When the Aborigines first tried to explain their ideas of creation to the white man, those who had learnt the white man's tongue found the word 'dream' to come nearest to what they meant by 'Alchera'. So we white people call the black man's 'Alchera' the Dream Time. We have also learnt that, besides applying the word 'Alchera' to the time of creation, the native uses it as well to stand for certain events in the Dream Time, which is why we have named our nine stations the nine Alchera.'

Rusking moistened his lips.

'In the Alchera, the Dream Time,' he resumed, 'the great culture hero, and there were many of him, one for almost every kind of tree, fruit, flower, insect, bird, animal and fish and also for sun, moon and stars, woke up from dreaming in a deep sleep and emerged from where he had been sleeping and dreaming – from under a pool, a mountain range, a tree, from the sky, the clouds, a star – and shook himself into complete consciousness. He was man-snake, man-lizard, man-bird, man-fish, man-fruit, man-insect or man-tree. He could be one, the man, this moment, the other – the animal, bird or plant – the next. He could be both at the same time.

'Fully awake, he armed himself with spears, throwing sticks and wooden dishes and set off on his journey. In the course of his travels, he formed mountains, rivers, valleys, waterholes, forests. They are there still for you to see. He created sons, he fashioned women and he initiated them into mysteries that you will witness later on. He created ceremonial poles that are still in his country as trees, columns of rocks, spire-like tors. The foes he slew can still be viewed in the form of huge boulders, mounds, and so on.

'Wherever he slept, he himself stayed for ever – more boulders, trees, tors – so that you can see your cultural hero in a hundred places, all equally sacred and important. Each is equally potent with spirit life so that today if a woman pauses nearby one of them a spirit particle will enter her and she will bear a child who is the mighty ancestor, the cultural hero himself.

'Finally, at the end of the journey, having created men and women of his own totem, the great hero died. You may still see him, if you are one of the initiated, in a massive rock preserved in a cave and protected from profane eyes.'

Corless realised that Julie Flax was standing beside him. He had no idea how long she had been there. She gave him a twitch of the mouth that might have been a smile.

He whispered, 'Carl Rusking tells me you're putting me up. Thanks very much. But please understand I had no idea of barging in on you when I cam here.'

Her expression became stormy.

'Your detective friend has no such inhibitions,' she said. 'He had the unmitigated nerve to say he *wanted* a room, that he would be staying until, well, as long as was necessary. It's unheard of.'

Corless reflected that Inspector Haig was probably capable of many unheard-of things.

'Why do you call him *my* friend?' he asked.

'You were talking to him cheek by jowl.'

Corless said, 'He's a policeman and he was talking about Laurie – '

Tourists close at hand turned and shushed indignantly and Corless subsided, red-faced.

Rusking was saying, 'Everything that exists now, animate or inanimate, lived in the Alchera or Dream Time. Everything fixed, like a rock, a mountain, a tree, was a living creature in the Alchera, is the physical vestige of a Dream Time hero or ancestor. Every bird, animal fish, insect or plant of today was in the Dream Time a cultural hero, a totem founder. Therefore, if your totem is Apma the Snake, you are the snake you see wriggling through the bush and the snake is you, and both of you are your Alchera ancestor.

'All these myths, traditions and beliefs,' continued Rusking, 'and many others are taught to the Aboriginal boy ready for manhood in a great festival called the 'Engwura' or 'Ingkura'.

So you see that as well as making a journey into the Dream Time, you are also taking part in the great *Engwura* rites. The real *Engwura* lasts for many months. Yours will last three or four hours. Consequently we have had to abridge any ceremonies and leave others out. Also, to give you a general picture, we have woven – most incorrectly, of course – the ceremonies of a *number* of totems into our *Engwura*. We are going to follow the adventures of Apma the Snake, but in them you will see events that really belong to *Ertwaitcha* the bell bird, *Indimita* the beetle, *Ilai* the emu, *Ungamillia* the evening star, and others.

'Now, ladies and gentlemen' – Rusking wiped his face with a handkerchief – 'a word of warning. There is one main path through Dream Time Land, the one on which you stand, but the Alchera stations are not on it – save one. They are placed on small side tracks in order to give them an atmosphere of secrecy and awe. The jungle bush is thick and dark. So please follow your guides. Don't wander off on your own.'

Rusking jumped down from the stump, and the didgeridoos came in strongly again. Austin Flax appeared holding back a creeper-covered branch. The tourists began to file through the narrow opening. Corless and Julie joined in the movement. Ahead, Corless distinguished the Winonga sergeant's big form. Slouch hats marked the position of constables in the crowd. The hunt was on.

Julie's mood had changed. 'Jock,' she said softly. 'Laurie was murdered, wasn't he?'

He twisted round so that he could look directly at her. 'Did Haig tell you that?'

'No.' She was nervous. 'It was Frank Bailey.'

'The young policeman. A friend of yours?'

'Yes,' said Julie slowly. 'You can call him a friend. A very good friend. Sometimes I think he's the only real friend I've got.'

'If you value him,' Corless said, 'don't let Haig know he told you. Have you told any of the others?'

She shook her head.

'Then don't. This Haig's tough.'

She leaned more closely to him. 'Does Haig suspect anybody?'

'Me, apparently,' said Corless bitterly.

'Oh, Jock, he can't! What did he say?'

But Corless had no chance to answer that question, for they had come to the creeper-covered branch and, ducking round it, they entered a path so narrow they had to walk in single file, which was the end of confidential talk.

The path twisted for thirty yards to open into a large tree-cavern so closed in and canopied by foliage it was like entering a dusky cave. No didgeridoos blared now. The tourists talked softly as though reluctant to disturb the gloomy hush.

'Over this way, please,' said Rusking's voice, and the crowd pressed towards one side where the darkness thickened so much that Corless suspected the presence of a grotto. In the jostling for position he lost contact with Julie.

'Alchera One,' said Rusking, now dimly visible. Behind him, Mallet reached up to a small switchboard. A faint orange glow shone within the darkness, revealing part of what seemed to be a still black pool.

'In the Alchera,' said Rusking, 'Apma the Snake lay sleeping beneath a pond of water. It was a time of nothing save sleeping heroes like Apma. As he slept, he dreamed of waking into magical life when all power would be his, the power to make and unmake, to create and obliterate, to make appear and disappear. And he dreamed of fashioning the ideal world for his descendants – a world of sun, food, water, women.'

Here, thought Corless, could be the source of Mrs Ashwood's dreams. Oddly enough, he saw her then. Her eyes were closed. She swayed as though in time to unheard music. One hand was on the arm of Martha Rea beside her.

'And then,' Rusking said, 'Apma awoke and began to struggle out of the pool.'

From an unseen loud-speaker came a roaring Aboriginal chant, rendered in English.

> *Apma came from earth!*
> *Apma came from water!*
> *Apma came from air!*
> *Earth and air and water Apma is!*
> *Apma, Oknirrabata! Wei!*

Mallet touched another switch, the light was stronger and the pool was seen in its entirety, though a few inches beyond its farther edge the blackness was still absolute. In the pool a dark, eerie, almost amorphous, form was visible. The only recognisable features were two strong, hard eyes that shone up through the water.

Corless wondered if the pool was real or if he was looking at a clever piece of painting. From that moment an uneasy sense of fantasy gripped him so that all that happened subsequently in that wild night seemed to have no hold on reality.

'This diorama,' said Rusking, 'like all that follow is a composite one. It shows Apma in various stages of his emergence from sleeping into wakefulness in the Dream Time. But snake or man, you are looking at Apma all the time.'

The light abruptly extended its bounds to show a wide stretch of yellow sand on which lay a great snake coiled round a nude, squatting blackfellow. Both were Apma the hero, but it was the snake you watched because of the power and wisdom of his eyes and lines of epic experience moulded into his head. And also sadness, thought Corless, as though Apma looked far ahead and saw destruction.

'Apma is awake,' Rusking said. 'But he is lonely and hungry. There is food to be got in the wide land around him, but it is not fitting that an *oknirrabata*, a supremely wise man, should get his own food. It is his sons' duty to feed him. But he has no sons. He has no wife to give him sons. So Apma calls on the magic he has been endowed with. He raises his right arm and plucks sons, fully grown, from his armpit.'

Back leaped the light and there was Apma, man and snake, and with him two fully grown sons. The man's right arm was outstretched and a third son was being taken from his armpit.

'Apma instructs his sons in the use of the throwing stick and the spear. He sends them out to catch some kangaroos grazing nearby. The sons return laden with meat. Apma teaches them how to make a fire, how to break and bind the kangaroo's legs, how to place them on the fire so that the fur is burnt off and the flesh baked. Then they sit down to the feast.'

Once more the orange light lifted back. Apma, the man and snake, sat by a fire, the sons courteously handing choice portions of meat to their father. In the fire two kangaroos were baking. Behind them was a rampart of steep, ribbed, flat-topped hills, red and brown and orange.

'The first feast in the Alchera,' said Rusking, 'is the first feast after the creation of the world. And this completes Alchera One.'

There was a moment's silence, broken by the sweet voices of lubras chanting to the clack of music sticks. The tourists began to clap. Corless, also applauding, looked at the hard, yellow, Central Australian scene. But his eyes kept coming back to the huge snake, to the terrible air of knowledge and power and sadness. There was an inner meaning in this if he could only get it.

Someone said, 'Mr Rusking, are you responsible for modelling these figures?'

'Under Austin Flax's guidance, yes.'

'Remarkable work,' said the voice, 'and a tremendous undertaking, the figures being life-size.'

Rusking smiled and stepped into the diorama. And then they realised how skilful had been the perspective and the use of lighting. With Rusking among them, the figures were seen to be no more than dolls.

The applause was tremendous. Someone near Corless said quietly, 'A lot of police here this afternoon.'

'Traffic control? Struth!' said the first speaker.

Stepping out of the diorama, Rusking said, 'Thank you. We'll go on to Alchera Two.'

But Corless did not move with the crowd. He heard a tiny whisper in his ear, felt a flutter on his neck. Simultaneously something struck into his collar and hung there, trembling.

CHAPTER 5

He took a quick glance round, but no one showed the slightest interest in him. He pulled the thing out and saw a piece of bone, sharp at one end, blunt at the other, and bound round the middle with strands of black fur or hair. He recognised it at once, a native pointing bone or death bone. But it was a bone with an innovation. Someone had feathered it to turn it into a dart.

The sharp end was sticky with some kind of liquid application. He was about to try the point with a finger when he noticed a girl making towards him. He pushed the bone into a pocket and fumbled round until he had it wrapped in a handkerchief.

The girl said diffidently, 'Mr Corless.'

He recognised Elsie Mannus, the waitress who claimed to be a friend of Laurie's. Her uniform was hidden under a dust coat. 'Yes?'

She said hesitantly, 'I don't want you to think I'm butting in, but I believe you've been talking about some money Laurie said he owed. Maybe I can help you.'

'You can! How?'

Her eyes went furtively to the people filing out of the glade.

'Not now,' she said. 'I'm not supposed to be here. There'd be trouble if I was seen. But Laurie used to talk to me and I took a chance to find you because I thought you'd go away after the show and I'd miss you.'

'There's an interval about four o'clock,' said Corless. 'And another later on.'

She shook her head. 'That's no good. I'm working during the intervals. But after the show has finished, I'll be free then. Do you know the cabins behind the cafe? Mine is number five. Could you meet me there, say about half-past nine?'

The top of her head was level with his shoulder, and she had to turn her face up to look at him. He noticed the droop of her lips. He guessed there were tears in her eyes. He did not think she would be drawing attention to herself if she had just thrown a feathered death bone at him.

Misinterpreting his glance, she said, 'This is not a try-on. I must talk to you about Laurie, I think I can explain those debts – I know I can – but I don't know what to do about them. Please say you'll come.'

'All right, I'll be there,' said Corless. 'Some time after half-past nine.'

'Thanks,' she said breathlessly. 'Now I must scoot or they'll be missing me.'

She went swiftly back towards the main entrance.

Corless hurried after the tail of the procession going to Alchera Two. Forty yards of deviously descending trail brought him to a second big, gloomy glade in the Dream Time Jungle. He saw tourists gathered on the far side but, just as he headed towards them, a hand gripped his arm and swung him into a dark pocket in the undergrowth.

'Our lady-killer at last,' said Haig's gravelly voice. 'And about time. Now we can get on with it.'

There were three people in the niche with Haig – Julie Flax, Carl Rusking and Ovid Mallet – but in the gloom Corless had to peer closely to recognise them.

'This is all very well, Inspector Haig,' said Rusking in disgruntled tones. 'But they're waiting for me over there. If I don't turn up soon, old Austin will get going and – '

'As a matter of fact, he will,' said Haig. 'I told him you'd be busy for a while.'

'Wouldn't it!,' groaned Rusking. 'Austin's all right, one of the best, but, dammit! He'll ruin the atmosphere. He hasn't got the touch.'

Even as he spoke, Austin's voice rose raucously. 'Folks, you're now goin' to view one of the most divertin' episodes in the Snake's progress. In Alchera One, y' seen how the Snake got sons because he was lonely and hungry. Well, he found he was still lonely. Sons is all right to get your tucker, but they don't keep y' warm at night. O' course, the Snake did what the black boys still do at night – make a little fire to curl round. But you can get burnt that way.' Austin paused thoughtfully. 'Come to think of it,' he said, 'you can get burnt other ways, too.'

There was a howl of laughter. Rusking was hopping mad.

'What did I tell you?' he protested to Haig. 'He just can't help it. One of the loveliest Alchera myths being smashed to hell! You've got no right to do this.'

'File this under Facts of Life,' growled Haig. 'I've got all the right when I'm hunting for a murderer.'

Corless thought that Julie's gasp was good acting. Rusking and Mallet were very still. In the pause, old Austin's voice was heard describing the efforts of Apma the Snake to make himself a wife. Through a break in the ranks of the tourists appeared a vista of the diorama; the reddish background of flat-topped ranges, the yellow sand, the snake and its alter ego, the black man, gazing at what looked like a whirlwind. From the darkest shadow of the jungle nook, Mallet's cold voice asked how Haig had concluded that Laurie Moore was murdered. Corless was scarcely aware of Haig's voice speaking of the evidence of Dr Lennox, the Winonga physician. He was again under the phantasmal spell of the Snake's terrible wisdom. Every line of Apma's scaly head seemed laden with hypnotic suggestion. He had the untenable feeling that the Snake knew.

'Cause of death a blow just behind the left ear which crushed the left parietal in,' said Haig. 'Weapon a club, a *nulla-nulla* like one of those hanging in the hall.'

Again silence. Haig began to roll a big, awkwardly shaped cigarette. Austin's voice rose stridently.

'So what does Apma do? He raises a whirlwind. A good 'un. It whirls the dust up into a solid column. Usin' his magic – wish I had it – he brings the whirlwind up to him an' cuts it down to size. Then, while it's whirlin' in front of him, he starts workin' on it with his hands. A touch here, a pat there, an' he's gettin' the shape he wants. The curves, swells, lines. Cripes, all of us blokes wish we had the same magic – '

Corless looked again at the diorama and saw the man-snake before a cleverly depicted dusty mass, through which showed the dark form of a lovely lubra.

Haig got his misshapen cigarette going.

'The man who drove the car' – he resumed and now his voice was part of the Dream Time alchemy – 'is a Mr David Wilson of Winonga. But any car would have done. Wilson's eyes are on the wet road, but even if they weren't, the scrub is thick on the embankment where the murderer waits in the mist and rain with a dead man propped up against him. The car comes and down goes Moore so that his death would look like an accident or, maybe, suicide.'

Haig paused and tapped the ash from his cigarette. His eyes watched the three people in front of him.

'It's the way things happen,' he said, 'that there was a police car close behind Wilson, that you, Miss Flax and Mr Mallet, should also be on the road, that Dr Lennox should be following soon after you. You'll remember that Sergeant Clough and his men were on their way to interview Moore.'

'You were with them,' said Julie.

'I was with them,' said Haig flatly.

'I wonder why?' said Mallet.

A sudden roar of mirth from Austin's audience had Rusking agonising like a martyr, but he heroically said nothing.

'I'll come back to that point,' said Haig. 'Also to why Sergeant Clough wanted to talk to Moore, for they're one and the same. But' – his crenellated jaw thrust out – 'you don't have to be told why the sergeant had a team with him.'

'Laurie was wild,' said Rusking with some regret. 'In the mood, he would take on anything in sight. Some time ago, he got into a brawl, and it took five policemen to subdue him.'

Long aware of his cousin's deplorable tendencies, Corless allowed his attention to flow back to the Snake. Once again the intuition that in the Snake's air of wisdom, of knowledge of good and evil, could be found the cause of Laurie's death rose in him. The horrible thing about this wisdom was its strange fascination. No wonder Mrs Ashwood dreamed.

Haig said, 'Moore was a brawler. Yet this tough bird, this vanquisher of policemen, five at a time, was killed by one man, and a small man at that.'

'How do you know that?' asked Julie, breathing hard.

'God's truth!' barked Haig. 'Isn't anything obvious in the world? Police do search the scene of a fatality. I climbed the bank behind the Well. Remember that it was raining. Despite the undergrowth and grass, I found the tracks of two men. I saw where they talked, where one fell. Then there were tracks of one man leading to the edge and the same tracks going away.'

He stopped and, to Corless, it seemed he waited with an avid expectancy. If so, he must have been disappointed.

Mallet sneered, 'Maybe. But how do we come into it?'

'Ah! The very question.' Haig dropped his cigarette and put his heel on it. 'Now I'll ask you something. When was the last time Moore went into town, Miss Flax?'

In the dim light, the purple eyes were dark hollows in which no gleam could be seen.

'That's difficult, Mr Haig. You didn't know Laurie. If he wanted to go anywhere, he went. He didn't ask permission. But the last time *I remember* him going to town was a fortnight ago.'

'According to Sergeant Clough, a fortnight is right,' said Haig triumphantly. 'You see, the police had cause to keep an eye on Moore, and they haven't seen him in town for a fortnight. Now they have a special reason for remembering that last occasion – '

'Laurie got into a fight as usual,' said Corless.

'The very reverse,' Haig chuckled. 'He had a few drinks but, instead of making him fight, the beer made him talk. He was with a drinking cobber called Jacks, and this is what he said to Jacks. "I'm in a hell of a mess, Jacks – "'

Corless started as heard the familiar phrase.

Haig continued, '"I'm on to a filthy game", said Moore to Jacks. "A game worse than murder. Somebody's going to do time over this, Jacks. But I can do nothing because I'll be doing time too, and I don't know how to get out of it."' Haig lit his second cigarette. '"It'd make your bloody hair stand on end, Jacks, if you knew what I know," said Moore to his mate. And that's all he did say, but Sergeant Clough heard about it. Add to that something else, and you have the reason why the sergeant and his men wanted to talk to Moore and why I was with them. Because, you see, the sergeant reported his ideas to Brisbane, and I was sent to look into the matter.'

A wondrous explosion of hilarity from the tourists had Rusking flinging up his arms.

'Haig,' he said desperately. 'I know all this is important, but will you let me get over there and save the wreckage?'

'No,' said Haig brutally.

'There was something else, inspector,' said Julie.

'You know the mailman who calls here?'

The girl nodded.

'Ten days ago,' said Haig, 'Moore gave that mailman a message for some storekeeper friend in Winonga. "Tell him," Moore said, "to collect all the money owing at Ungamillia before the place blows to hell."'

'Oh, no!' Julie cried. 'Laurie could never have said that. It's unthinkable. There's nothing at Ungamillia – '

'The mailman will swear to it', said Haig. 'And now we come to Laurie Moore's cousin. The feller standing here.

Moore wrote a letter to him asking for help, even though they hadn't been friends for years. Moore told his cousin he was in a hell of a mess. Note the words. He asked his cousin to come six hundred miles to see him. He made a rendezvous. He would be at the Well of St Giles every day for a week between the hours of twelve and one. And then, in case anything happened, he enclosed a statement of money owing to various people. Which brings me to the real nub of the way things happen. Two people want to see Moore urgently. His cousin for one. I'm the other. And he is murdered before either of us can see him.'

Over at the diorama, the background Aboriginal chanting had started again. The scene had changed and the Snake was bigger and stronger.

Haig took Laurie's list from his pocket. Because it was dark in this jungle corner, he flicked on his cigarette lighter, held it close to the page and read the statement through.

> *Carl Rusking ... £212. 13. 1*
> *Mrs Ashwood ... £1,131. 9. 1*
> *Martha Rea ... £2,120. 1. 1*
> *Ovid Mallet ... £1,118. 9. 1*
> *Austin Flax ... £220. 11. 1*
> *Julie Flax ... £21. 13. 1*

Haig stopped and Austin Flax's voice filled the gap. 'Folks, in Central Australia whirlwinds is dangerous things to this day. They still have the magic put in 'em by Apma the Snake. When a lubra sees one comin', she ups an' runs for her life. She knows, o' course, if the whirlwind gets her, there's another little Apma on the way, and, gosh! she's got enough already –'

'Haig,' said Rusking, almost weeping. 'You heard that. I've got to get over there and – '

'No,' snarled Haig. 'About these debts – '

Rusking was suddenly angry.

'Jock has already gone into that. There is no money owing.

At least, not to anybody on that list. Not to anybody at Ungamillia.'

'Then what does the list mean?'

Corless had asked himself that question a score of times. He was also asking himself if the inspector had now removed him from the list of suspects. A third problem intruded – the dark way in which Julie watched him. He had told her that he merely happened to be here. It was as though the invisible coils of Apma the Snake were closing on him.

Haig said, 'I've got two possibilities. The first is the murderer came from Ungamillia.'

'That's one of the most horrible things I've ever heard,' said Rusking.

'But logical,' Haig pointed out. 'So logical I'm going to ask each of you to say where you were between eleven o'clock and twelve o'clock this morning.'

'For me that's easy,' said Rusking, with the air of one wanting to get it over quickly. 'From ten o'clock to about a quarter to one I was here in Dream Time Land. I've got ten thousand pounds' worth of gear here, and I've got to watch it. I was going round all the stations. They're under weatherproof canopies, but I had to make sure the rain wasn't getting in. Now you know about me, inspector.'

'Any supporting evidence?'

Rusking was taken aback, but he recovered quickly.

'I'd forgotten that,' he admitted. 'I was up at the house about twenty-past twelve, maybe a bit later, and Ovid and Julie came in with the news about poor Laurie. They said they'd seen you down at the Well. You see, you're a ringer for Laurie, Jock. But I didn't know you were coming. I only knew you when I saw you.'

Rusking turned to Haig. 'Can I go now?'

'Wait on,' said Haig, scowling. 'When did you last see Moore?'

'At breakfast. About eight o'clock.'

'And you've got no proof you were here between eleven and twelve?'

'None at all. And I'm not worried. But I am worried about old Austin. Listen to that.'

The tourists were rocking with laughter. All the sombre, awesome effect built up at Alchera One had been blown away in gales of mirth.

Haig had pity. 'Okay, clear off. But I haven't finished with you yet. You had a queer lapse of memory, Mr Rusking.'

But Rusking paid no attention. He sped across the glade, shouldered through the crowd and Austin's cracked voice stopped abruptly.

Haig looked at Julie. 'Your turn, Miss Flax.'

'From half-past ten to half-past eleven,' said the girl, a suggestion of a wobble in her voice, 'I was in Winonga, shopping and doing other things. And you must remember this goes for Ovid, too, for he was with me. We left for home about 11.30, as I said, and we arrived at the Well a minute or two after the police car.'

'Evidence?'

Over at the diorama, Rusking's voice rose quietly and persuasively. The real myth of Apma and the whirlwind was being told.

'For me, the manager of the Bank of Australia,' said Mallet stiffly. 'I had a deal of business to put through. As for Julie – '

'Let her speak for herself.'

'A number of people,' Julie said. 'Storekeepers. But I had to renew my driving licence, so I'd best refer you to Frank Bailey.'

'Bailey? Oh-oo!' Haig's voice developed an edgy irony. 'Ask a friendly policeman, eh? Okay, I'll ask him. And I guess that's enough for – '

'Just a moment,' interposed Mallet acidly. 'Isn't there something you've forgotten? What about those tracks? Either they came back to Ungamillia or they didn't.'

'Yair, the tracks,' said Haig. He appeared to be uncomfortable. 'There was one set came down from Ungamillia –

Moore's. Hard to follow through the scrub. Then another set came in from the right as you face down hill. That's the west. Moore's prints never went back. But the other set followed back to where they came in from the west, then returned to a huge clump of scrub and creeper and fallen trees. And there both sets vanished. The reason is simple. The timber is so thick you could easily do a Tarzan act through it.'

'So,' said Mallet, crowing, 'your second possibility. The murderer came from *outside* Ungamillia!'

'Keep going,' Haig growled.

'I happen to know who made those tracks,' said Mallet viciously. 'A man who was on the scene at the Well and yet never said a word about himself. Mr Corless.'

Corless found Haig's hand restraining him.

'Finish it,' the detective said.

'I certainly will.' Mallet took a deep breath. 'Mr Corless is armed with a letter alleged to be from his cousin and also a statement of alleged debts. The letter purports to make certain arrangements for a meeting. Now I happen to know there was bad feeling between Mr Corless and his cousin. You reminded us, inspector, that Moore liked to talk. Suppose Mr Corless did keep his appointment an hour earlier than the letter arranges? Suppose Mr Corless met Moore, killed him, threw him in front of Wilson's car, then sneaked away, got into his own car and arrived innocently after the "accident" had occurred?'

Haig said, 'I seem to have heard something about a strange black.'

'Now you're talking in riddles,' Mallet retorted.

Corless's memory flipped a shutter open, and he thrust hard at Mallet.

'That snap you dropped in the cafe. It showed a naked black and a naked white man, too.'

'Are you mad?' said Mallet.

'You dropped a photograph. I picked it up. You snatched it out of my hand.'

'You're a stupid liar,' Mallet said contemptuously. 'There was no – '

Corless lunged forward, but Haig's grip was like iron.

'Just a moment,' said the detective, hauling Corless back.

'Who,' he demanded, 'altered the sign at the junction?'

Rusking's voice rose murmurously in the silence that followed.

Finally Mallet said, 'I did. I'll tell you why. I told Julie why when I did it. I recognised Corless at the Well because of his likeness to his cousin. But he didn't speak or reveal himself. I felt there was something queer about the "accident". I guessed that Corless would be on his way to Ungamillia. I wanted to delay him so that I could discuss his being at the Well with Julie and Rusking. And it did delay him. Afterwards I went down and put the sign right.'

'Okay with you, Miss Flax?'

It was very dark in the jungle pocket now, but Julie seemed badly disturbed.

'Yes.'

'There could be another reason for changing the sign,' said Haig. 'That back way in is a dangerous proposition when it's wet. Suppose you didn't want Corless to arrive at all, eh? What about that?'

'Oh, no, no!' Julie cried. 'Nothing of the sort.'

'Well, another reason still,' pursued Haig. 'You wanted to talk about Corless. Not about whether he did his cousin in, but whether he could be suspecting somebody up here killed him. And what precautionary measures to take.'

'Completely wrong,' said Julie desperately.

'Then what did you discuss?'

'I'll tell you,' said Mallet savagely. 'We discussed Martha Rea. For she is the reason why Corless killed his cousin. She was becoming too friendly with Moore.'

'Yes, a good motive,' said Haig. 'So good that we've got to do something about it.'

The detective whistled softly and Sergeant Clough, hardly

recognisable in the gloom, came into the recess so promptly that he must have been waiting nearby. Corless felt very cold.

'Sergeant,' said Haig. 'You have rung the motel at Benogra?'

'Yes, I spoke to the proprietor,' the sergeant replied. 'He said he clearly recalled a man driving a steel-grey Goddess. He described the man. It was Mr Corless without any doubt. He said that after eating and buying petrol Mr Corless left there on the tick of ten o'clock.'

'How long, driving fast, would it take to get here from Benogra?'

'Driving your best on that road, two hours.'

'Mr Mallet', said Haig. 'You saw Corless arrive. What was the time?'

Mallet did not speak, but Julie said, 'I saw him. It was a minute or two after twelve o'clock.'

'Mallet,' said Haig gloomily, 'if you'd listened to what I told you, you wouldn't have wasted my time. I said the murder was committed by a small man. And I also said the murderer's tracks came from the west. Corless, driving from Benogra, came from the south-east, and how in Hades he could have got his car round that traffic block I do not know. Corless is out for the same reason you and Miss Flax are out.'

He released Corless's arm. Corless took one step forward, driving his fist straight and hard, and Mallet hurried into the scrub behind him.

'I didn't see a thing,' said Haig. 'Did you sergeant?'

'Not a thing,' said the sergeant solemnly.

'What about you, Miss Flax?'

After a pause, Julie, speaking in a stifled voice, said, 'No, I saw nothing.'

CHAPTER 6

The rhythm of a corroboree dance pulsated from Alchera Three, drawing the tourists eagerly down a steep, tunnel-like passage through the jungle. But Haig and Corless did not immediately follow the procession.

Gazing into the orange light which showed how Apma the Snake got himself a wife, Corless felt the tingling in his knuckles gradually abate. The unnerving influence of the Snake's eyes was on him again. Carl Rusking was an artist of extraordinary potency.

Haig said quietly, 'Who was the girl talking to you back at Alchera One?'

'You don't miss much, do you?' said Corless. 'That girl was Elsie Mannus, a waitress at the cafe. She wanted – '

He stopped as full memory returned.

'Wanted what, Jock?'

Corless gave an account of his conversation with the girl.

'We'll be there at half-past nine,' said Haig.

'We?'

'If she'll talk to you, she'll talk to me.' Haig's chest swelled perceptibly. 'I'm not unpopular with women. I have charm.'

In the yellow light, his gargoyle features had all the charm of a Papuan witch-doctor. Corless eyed him sourly.

'Perhaps you can use your charm to explain this,' he said. 'Perhaps it was *my* charm that made someone shy it at me.'

He took out his handkerchief and unwrapped the feathered death bone.

Haig examined the tacky nature of the substance on the point with unusual delicacy.

'This stick into you?'

'No. It caught in my collar.'

The detective went noiselessly into the jungle where the beam of his torch presently appeared glancing through the tangle of scrub and trees. When he emerged a little later, he carried a small tree frog.

'Give me that thing,' he said.

The unfortunate frog squirmed as he made a small incision under its left foreleg with the pointed end of the bone. The squirming suddenly changed into convulsions which were more than Haig could control without tearing the creature's soft flesh. He put it on the ground where it continued to writhe until it collapsed on its back. From incision to death was less than sixty seconds.

'Poor old frog,' said Haig. 'That wasn't kind, but something had to be done quickly.'

Picking the frog up, he took it to the fringe of the bush and placed it under a log. He came back to Corless.

'Somebody doesn't like you, Jock,' he said. 'This bone's tipped with snake venom. At a guess, taipan. It will take Dr Lennox to find out.'

Corless was conscious of icy shivers in his stomach. 'Why should anybody want to kill me?' he said.

Haig's ugly face slipped into sly angles. 'Suppose someone thinks you know more than you say you do? Suppose they reckon you *do* know the meaning of your cousin's debts?'

'But I don't.'

'But suppose you do?'

And now Haig's face was no longer sly but hard and demanding.

'Digger, I'll say it again,' said Corless, exasperated. 'I don't know what they mean.'

Down at Alchera Three, a chorus sang of Apma, the great creator.

> *Apma pointed the spear;*
> *Tall were green trees.*
> *Apma dragged the spear;*
> *Sweet flowed cold water.*
> *Apma lifted the spear;*
> *Mountains leaped from earth.*
> *Apma, Oknirrabata! Wei!*

Haig listened, his head nodding in time to the chant. He re-wrapped the death bone in Corless's handkerchief and put the little packet in his pocket.

'We'll see what this Elsie Mannus has to say.' He pondered a moment, then added, 'A pretty kid. Let us descend, Jock.'

The tourists stood in the circle of orange light, their eyes on the figures of Apma, man and snake, who faced away over yellow sand towards a darkness-shrouded background.

'You must imagine,' said Rusking, 'the formless kind of world into which Apma awoke. There was earth without form, trees that were not fixed, stars that roamed as you watched, water that broke all the laws of science. There were man-animals, animal-men. There were the sun and moon without places, winds that did not know how or where to blow. There were all the elements of a world, but the world had to be brought into form and reduced to order.

'This was Apma's great magic, the power to produce the world he wanted – his ideal world. Not the ideal world for you or me, but the ideal world for the blackfellow, based on five points: food, warmth, shelter, companionship, freedom from strange magic.'

Rusking paused, then he said, 'Not so different from our ideal world, after all. So Apma goes to work.'

An unseen light flicked on, and there was Apma the Snake

wriggling across a wide expanse, leaving a river behind him as his trail.

'Water to drink and deep water-holes for fish.'

Another sector lighted up, and there was Apma the man casting up a mountain chain.

'Peaks where one can gaze across a mighty stretch of sunlit country and become as wide and wise and grand as the view itself.'

'Hold on a moment,' Haig muttered, as if to himself. 'There's something here I've missed.'

Section after section of the diorama came into the orange light. Apma slicing gaps in the mountain range so that water could run through and his people have cool refuges from summer heat; Apma setting up places for witchetty grubs, kangaroos, lizards, honey-ants, yelka-nuts, yams, so that the tribe, moving around, would always have food.

'By now,' said Rusking, 'it is becoming evident to you that the blackfellow's myth is an expression of the universal desire for a world without fear, stress, disaster, death. In his myth, he is striving for the world he wants. And' – Rusking paused – 'aren't we all?'

A languourous voice near Corless murmured:

> 'Ah, Love! could thou and I with Fate conspire
> To grasp this sorry Scheme of Things entire,
> Would not we shatter it to bits – and then
> Re-mould it nearer to the Heart's Desire!'

Corless took one glance at the soft round face just seen in the orange light. The eyes were closed. The lips continued to move silently.

'The dreamer,' said Haig.

But Corless looked beyond Mrs Ashwood at Martha Rea. She resolutely watched the diorama, but he knew from the scornful set of her lips that she was aware of his presence.

Rusking resumed his narration. From the darkness on the opposite side of the glade came a little chirrup as though a jungle insect had just wakened up. Haig put his hand on Corless's shoulder and pulled him quietly away from the crowd.

Two men waited in the thick gloom. One wore the slouch hat of a policeman. Peering closely, Corless saw that the other was Austin Flax.

'I got him,' said the policeman.

'Thanks, Bailey,' said Haig. Then, as the earnest young constable began to move away, he spoke again. 'Just a moment.'

'Yes, sir?'

'Miss Flax has given your name as a referee concerning her movements in Winonga this morning.'

'I've been expecting that,' said Bailey. 'Yes, I can vouch for her time in Winonga. Most of it, anyway. She had to renew her driving licence, and it took some time. You needn't worry about Julie, inspector.'

'I'm not worrying about anybody,' Haig said testily. 'Very well, you can get back on the job.'

Constable Bailey walked away quietly. His hat became one of the half-dozen slouch hats silhouetted against the diorama's glow.

'Well, old party,' Haig said to Austin. 'It's your turn to talk.'

'What about?' demanded Austin belligerently.

'They tell me,' said Haig, 'you spent most of the morning digging a hole in front of the house and singing "Onward Christian Soldiers".'

'Yair. An' I spent a lot of the afternoon singin' "Onward Christian Soldiers" an' fillin' the hole in. But I know what you want. I was workin' on the hole from about ten o'clock till about twelve, an' then I had me lunch – you can ask Kitty Winn about that. An' then Genghiz Khan got loose, an' I had to chase him. You can ask the young feller here about that.'

'Who is Kitty Winn?'

'One o' the girls at the cafe. An' a real bouncy sport, too.'

Austin chuckled. 'She'll tell y' how long I took over me lunch. As for the mornin', I reckon that dreamin' Ashwood dame will tell y' I was diggin' all the time. Maybe she won't though. She don't like me. An' I don't like her, neither. I s'pose you haven't changed your mind about Laurie bein' murdered?'

'It was murder, old party.'

Austin sighed. 'Damn' hard. I liked that boy. He had real life an' guts. Why, I seen him handle five policemen, which is why Sergeant Clough was bringin' out a mob today. An' I reckon there's another boy here just as good.'

He pushed a thumb towards Corless. 'I'll lay sixes,' said Haig, 'I can put Jock on his back any time I like.'

'Done!' said Austin fiercely. 'I haven't seen a real stoush since Laurie belted the Johns in Winonga.'

'Country coppers!' jeered Haig. And then his manner became serious. He turned his back to the crowd, drew Austin and Corless close to him, felt in his pockets and, the next moment, under cover of his coat his torch shone on the feathered death bone. 'Ever seen that before?' he asked Austin.

'One of mine,' said the old man promptly. 'How did you get it? An' who the hell's been stickin' feathers on it?'

'Sure it's one of yours?'

'O' course,' Austin snorted. 'Bucktooth Tommy give me that bone.'

'And who's Bucktooth Tommy?' asked Haig, putting torch and bone away.

'A camel boy I had back in the Centre.' The old man's tone became reminiscent. 'I remember how he come to give it to me, too. Twenty-five year ago, now. I'm comin' in from the Mann Ranges, makin' for Oodnadatta, ridin' one camel an' leadin' another, an' behind the led camel is Bucktooth, paddin' along on foot. We come to a patch o' mulga scrub, see, an' I'm singin' "Onward Christian Soldiers". It's me theme song. I remember readin' somethin' about the bloke who wrote it, a feller called Sabine Brin'-Gould. There's a name for y'. Sabine. Cripes, it's the Sabine women them ancient Romans raped. How'd a bloke get a name like that?'

'About this death bone,' said Haig.

'Yair. It's a warm afternoon, an' Bucktooth's half asleep on his feet. An' right behind him comes the biggest flamin' dingo you ever seen. Just sniffin' along behind Bucktooth's heels, curious. Meant no harm, see. Just wanted to find out what the corset's all about.'

'Corset?' said Corless.

'Cortege,' said Haig. 'Keep going, old party.'

'Yair,' said Austin. 'I'm singin' "Onward Christian Soldiers" see? Without stoppin', I get me revolver out, a thirty-eight. I'm still singin' an' I turn round in the saddle an' take a couple of shots at the dingo just behind Bucktooth. Well, damme! I'm singing' like this:

'"Like a mighty har-r- – ha-mee-e – BANG! –

'Moves the Church – BANG! – God-d-d – "

'The dingo whizzes round an' lights out so fast Bucktooth never seen him. Poor coot thinks I'm shootin' at him, an' he takes off about a hundred mile an hour, too. I yell me head off, but he don't come back, so I go an' make camp. An' that night, I'm sittin' over the fire, an' I hear somethin' move in the scrub, an' I sing out, "Come on, you dam' fool, Bucktooth! I wasn't shootin' at you. Come an' get your munga." He sidles out of the mulga an' says, "Yair, boss. But, boss, no more Clistmiss Soldier, boss." An' the next day, he gives me this here bone. "That'll stop the Clistmiss soldier, boss," he says. But, o' course, it never did.'

Haig grinned. 'So the bone is yours, old party, eh? Well, who's the stray black wandering around Ungamillia?'

'If there is one, he ain't Bucktooth,' replied the old man. 'Bucktooth died o' measles fifteen year ago in the Alice. Anyway, somebody's swingin' on your hoof. There's only them models of Carl's here.'

'When did you see Laurie Moore last?'

'Just after I started diggin' this mornin'. He stood an' watched me a while an' roughed ol' Genghiz Khan up a bit. A real dag, Laurie.'

'What was the last thing he said to you?'

Austin was silent for ten seconds or so. When he spoke his manner was troubled.

'Laurie don't sound like himself. "I'm gettin' restless ol' feller," he tells me. "Reckon the time's comin' when I got to pull out." I says, "Y' can't do that to me, Laurie. You think it over." "I've thought it over," he says. "It looks like I got to go."'

'And so?' prompted Haig.

'When I heard what happened down at the Well,' Austin replied, 'I thought he meant he was goin' to do himself in. In a way, it's better to know somebody got him instead.'

Haig said, 'Somebody here got him.'

'No.'

'Yes. You wanted to know who feathered the bone. I don't know, but somebody threw it at Jock a few minutes ago. It stuck in his collar, else he'd have been a dead man. The point is smeared with snake venom that killed a frog in just under sixty seconds.'

The old man stood rigidly still for what seemed a long time, then he stumbled away. Haig let him go four paces, then he spoke sharply. 'Austin!'

'Yair?'

'Just one more matter. Julie isn't really your daughter, is she?'

'Who's been talkin' to you?' Austin demanded fiercely.

Haig said, 'I knew four days ago I was coming to Ungamillia. I always try to find out as much as I can about people before I start anything. I rang Alice Springs. The police told me you were never married.'

'Any harm in a man adoptin' a kid?' rasped the old man. And when Haig refrained from comment, he went on, 'She's the daughter of Charlie Armstrong, one of me best friends in the Territory. Her mother died when she was a baby an' Charlie disappeared when she was four.'

'Disappeared?'

'Took a trip into Simpson's Desert an' never come back. You can guess what happened. An' what's wrong with me adoptin' her?'

'Nothing whatsoever,' said Haig.

Within the jungle gloom, Alchera Three was a small bright universe in which Apma the Snake studded a blue-black sky with golden stars. Rusking's pleasant voice told of the hidden meaning of Apma's creative magic. There was no other sound until Sergeant Clough brought Mrs Ashwood and Martha Rea to where Haig and Corless waited. Mrs Ashwood was indignant. Every moment in Dream Time Land had its peculiar significance, and she did not want to miss a thing. She thought Haig unpleasantly officious.

Haig replied that what Mrs Ashwood thought was of no interest to him – file that under Salutary Lessons – and then went on to question her and Martha, whom he called Florence or Nightingale or both, on their movements in the morning and when they had last seen Laurie Moore.

If he gained anything of value from them, Corless missed it. He was intensely aware of Martha, though in the dusk her face was only a pale blur and her eyes unlit shadows. He was aware, too, of her perfume. It was called 'Mystique'. He knew it well because he had bought bottles of it, and it had cost him a whack of money. The association between the perfume and himself apparently meant nothing to her. A normal-minded girl would have hurled the stuff away and never used it again.

He cast back, wondering just *what* had gone wrong between them. Small things at first, he recalled. She wanted to go out and he didn't. He wanted to go fishing, and she had other ideas. She thought the old home behind the store ought to be burnt down, and he thought it was good enough for anybody, including her. He thought a new hat was an abomination, and she thought he didn't know what he was talking about.

That was the kind of thing. Nothing serious, he allowed. But the sum total was serious. It grew and multiplied until there was a blazing row that left behind a mountain of pride as hard as fused rock. That pride of hers! He was proud, too, but a man was entitled to his pride.

'Mrs Ashwood,' Haig was saying. 'What was the last thing Moore said to you?'

'I rarely spoke to him,' said Mrs Ashwood distantly.

'I don't care if your words to him were as rare as grasshoppers at the South Pole,' said Haig. 'What was the last thing he said to you?'

'"Pass the salt",' said Mrs Ashwood. 'At breakfast this morning. I passed the salt.'

Haig was silent for some disgruntled moments, then he turned to Martha. 'The last thing he said to you, Nightingale?'

'I wouldn't remember.'

'Come, come, Florence. Didn't he speak to you this morning? I understand he was a friend of yours.'

'He was not a friend of mine,' said Martha. 'And I made sure he didn't speak to me this morning.'

'O-ho! Aha-a!' said Haig, giving a passable imitation of Victor Borge. 'Well, what was the last thing you said to *him*?'

Martha said she hadn't the faintest idea.

'Of course you have,' put in Mrs Ashwood tartly. 'The last thing you said to him was, "*Take that!*" The night before last. I was there and heard you. And I don't suppose, Martha, any man's ever had his face smacked like Laurie Moore then.'

Corless found he had a curiously warm tingle in his skin.

Haig was delighted. 'You smacked his face! Why, Nightingale?'

'I refuse to discuss it,' said Martha, in the tone which Corless had reason to know meant that no power within his experience could force her to change her mind.

Haig waited for Mrs Ashwood to provide the explanation, but the slumbrous lady was suddenly unco-operative. She had turned towards the glow of the diorama. She listened to Rusking's voice. Corless saw that dreams were back in her eyes.

'How long have you been at Ungamillia?' asked Haig.

Mrs Ashwood was stubbornly silent, so Martha supplied the answer.

'Two months.'

'A holiday?'

Martha explained that Mrs Ashwood was convalescing after a serious illness.

Haig then began a series of questions concerning how they occupied their time at Ungamillia. At first Corless listened indifferently, and then, realising where these questions led, he was suddenly badly disturbed. How did they fill in their evenings, for instance? Well, there were occasional trips to the pictures at Winonga; there were books to read and games and music.

What kind of games?

The usual thing; bridge, solo, chess, table tennis – all sorts of pastimes.

'What about darts?' asked Haig carelessly.

Yes, they played darts.

'And who's the champion?' pursued Haig silkily.

'They're all pretty fair at the game,' said Martha with some reserve.

Mrs Ashwood came out of her self-imposed isolation.

'Oh, don't be so modest,' she said to Martha. 'You can give anybody a start of seventy and beat them hands down.'

In Corless, who recalled Martha's superlative skill with darts, rose an icy sensation. At the diorama Rusking was making some announcement, but he missed it.

'Very interesting,' said Haig from the corner of his mouth.

'Why?' demanded Mrs Ashwood.

'I'm looking for a champion dart-thrower. One threw a dart at Jock a while ago. A peculiar kind of dart. It was a death bone tipped with snake-poison.'

Haig walked away into the darkness as he spoke. At the same time, the familiar *wah*, *wah* and *wei*, *wei*, *wei* of a corroboree wailed from the concealed speaker and the tourists broke into jumbled movement. With them went Mrs Ashwood, everything but the wondrous allegory of Dream Time Land forgotten. Thus it came about that Corless was alone with Martha without quite understanding how it happened.

The chanting ceased, leaving only the noise of the tourists tramping through the jungle. Now that they had gone, the orange light reached unimpeded across the glade. It showed the taut, desperate look on Martha's face.

'Jock Corless,' she said between clenched teeth. 'Do you think I threw a poisoned dart at you?'

He said gloomily, 'I wouldn't be surprised at anything you do.'

Her hand landed on his face just one-quarter of a second later. If the smack Laurie had got from her was anything like this, his head must have rung for hours. Corless reeled. Martha whirled and ran, but he caught her in five steps and spun her round to face him.

'Let me go!' she panted and kicked at him.

He found a grip on her elbows that held her still.

'Listen,' he said. 'You hate me and I'm damned if I think much of you, but I deserved that. I apologise.'

She fought against his grip unavailingly.

'I'll tell you something,' he went on, breathing heavily. 'I hit Mallet a while back. Socked him on the jaw. He said I was the one who killed Laurie, but that wasn't why I hit him. I hit him because he brought your name into it.'

She did not speak, but she gave up trying to pull away and he thought he could safely release her.

Continuing, he said, 'He implied you were the reason for the killing. So you see, I didn't mean what I said. I'm sorry I said it. But' – a whiff of 'Mystique' came to him – 'by thunder, you irritate a man!'

'You're loathsome,' she said. 'How I wish I'd never met you or Laurie Moore either.'

This time he let her go, but she went the wrong way, taking the path that returned to Alchera Two. Watching with some bewilderment, he became aware of a silence so profound he could have been alone in Dream Time Land. The diorama still glowed redly and the uncanny eyes of Apma the Snake stared at him.

Then he fairly jumped. Inspector Haig came picking his way through the diorama, a giant – a golden giant – in comparison with Rusking's models.

'First intermission, Jock,' the detective said, carefully stepping out from the diorama. 'You were too busy with Florence to notice Brother Rusking's announcement.' He peered at Corless's face. 'She belted you a beaut, son. But no matter. I've no doubt she'll make up for it, though if she hadn't landed you I'd have had the handcuffs rattling.'

'Apart from watching me,' said Corless stiffly, veering away from the distasteful subject of Martha Rea, 'what have you been doing?'

Haig did not reply directly. He stood with one hip hunched, his hands in his pockets, his coat open and drawn back so that his broad chest bulged defiantly. He gazed round the glade as though he suspected that someone watched and listened. Then he took out Laurie Moore's statement of alleged debts and held it so that the orange light fell clearly over the names and amounts.

Corless studied them again, even though every figure was cut deep into his memory.

> Carl Rusking ... £212. 13. 1
> Mrs Ashwood ... £1,131. 9. 1
> Martha Rea ... £2,120. 1. 4
> Ovid Mallet ... £1,118. 9. 1
> Austin Flax ... £220. 11. 1
> Julie Flax ... £21. 13. 1

'I've been thinking about this,' said Haig. His face was cool, grave, earnest, giving no suggestion of his normal cock-a-hoop style. He was, as it were, stripped for action. 'Your cousin,' he went on, 'told you to study the figures carefully if anything should happen. In this list' – Haig shook the paper – 'there's a message in cipher.'

'A devilishly complicated cipher, then.'

'I don't think so,' said Haig. He bent into the diorama and hauled out two camp stools. 'We'll sit straight down, Jock, and get at this thing. We're beaten until we know why your cousin was killed. I believe this list will tell us why. I think I know how it works and we've got an hour. Enough for clever blokes like us to break it,' he added with the ghost of a grin.

Corless sat down with some mental reservations. He would not have chosen Alchera Three, or any other Alchera for that matter, as the venue for the exercise of pure logic.

Haig had an open notebook on his knee, but he did not settle to work at one. He gazed into the diorama and chewed the end of his pencil.

'A queer place,' he muttered. 'Queer minds produced it. I've got to keep telling myself that snake is only a thing of painted plastic with electric bulbs for eyes ... Jock' – he tapped the statement – 'we forget the names of the debtors. We forget the amounts as money. We treat them simply as a list of digits. Like this.'

He wrote rapidly:

```
2 1 2 1 3 1 1 1 3 1 9
1 2 1 2 0 1 4 1 1 1 8
9 1 2 2 0 1 1 1 2 1 1
3 1
```

'My bet,' he said, 'is this is a very simple cipher. In the circumstances, your cousin didn't have time to work out anything complicated. Besides, he had enough intelligence not to make it tough. He wanted it understood quickly, but he turned it into pounds, shillings and pence and stuck names against it to lead wrong people off the track. So I'm guessing he wrote down the alphabet and stuck a number against each letter. He could have started with 1 for A, 2 for B, and so on till he came to 26 for Z. Or he could have reversed the procedure – 26 for A, 25 for B, and so on. But go for the first because, if you look at the list, you see a lot of ones which, in the second alternative, would mean a lot of zeds. Of course, he could have worked out some arbitrary arrangements of letters and numbers. If he did, we're shot, for he left no key as far as I can tell.'

The pressure of time showed on Haig's face as he said this.

'Or he could have used the numbers 1 to 26 consecutively,' said Corless, getting into the game, 'but started anywhere along the line, such as 15 for A, 16 for B, and finishing with 14 for Z. How do you know which one to pick?'

'Trial and error,' said Haig grimly. He looked round the jungle background as if searching for someone. Then he returned to the list of digits. 'But, if you study the figures, you see nineteen ones, seven twos and just a few other digits. So I think we can start with 1 for A.'

He turned a page and wrote the letters of the alphabet, numbering each one. He tore the leaf out.

'You hold this, Jock. It'll save time and trouble looking for corresponding numbers. Now let's take the first eight digits and see what we get.'

On a third leaf, he wrote the first eight figures and under each a corresponding letter with this result:

```
2  1  2  1  3  1  1  1
B  A  B  A  C  A  A  A
```

'And that,' he said, his eyes glinting yellow, 'is gibberish. We'll try 'em in pairs. 21, 21, 31. U, U – and there's no 31, of course. Okay. We'll grant the first figure is alone and that some of the others are paired. For instance, 12 could be L. Now how do we go?'

After some varied efforts, he produced the following:

```
2  12  1  3  11
B  L   A  C  K
```

This made sense. Three minutes later, when he made a

further addition, it seemed he really was on the track. He now had:

```
2  12  1  3  11  13  1  9  12
B   L  A  C   M   A  I  L
```

An ominous word. Corless looked at his watch. Twenty-three minutes of the hour had gone. At this rate, the cipher would be resolved with time to spare. But Haig's early good fortune was not to be continued, for every combination he tried thereafter resulted in nonsense.

Time scampered. Any moment now and the tourists would be back to resume the adventures of Apma the Snake. Haig's notebook filled with arrangements of the remaining digits in pairs and singletons until it seemed he had exhausted every combination. Normally, he would have yielded to angry profanity, but his expression hardened and thinned and the lines of his face became rigid.

Finally he put down his notebook and stared into the diorama, his eyes reflecting the orange light.

'We're beaten, Jock. And that damned snake seems to know it. Yet I know we're on the track. The first word proves that. Dammit, it must come out. It's got to come out.'

Then he thumped his knee. 'Of course, fool, of course,' he said, and Corless restrained an impulse to laugh. 'Who said it should *all* be in English? Dream Time Land! This is a blackfellow's game.'

He started again, working swiftly. But time was on the blink. Voices sounded in the jungle above them and the first of the tourists, returning from the cafe, edged into the glade. They gazed curiously at the two sitting so intently before the diorama and one, a man, came over with the hearty intention of joining in whatever fun was going.

'Friend,' said Haig with unusual restraint, 'we're busy. Kindly remove yourself.'

The fellow retreated, affronted, and thereafter they were left to themselves. Five minutes later – the trickle of returning tourists had grown to a steady stream – Haig pushed the final result at Corless and muttered, 'Look at it, Jock, and let your hair stand on end as your cousin told the fellow, Jacks.'

2	12	1	3	11	13	1	9	12		1	20	14	1
B	L	A	C	K	M	A	I	L		A	T	N	A

1	18	9	12	20	1		11	21	13	1
A	R	I	L	T	A		K	U	M	A

'What are the last three words?' asked Corless, still unenlightened.

Haig stood up and gazed round the assemblage. His manner was mild, somewhat melancholy.

He said, 'It's one of the aspects of Myall life that is never mentioned. Not many people know about it, and just as well, too.'

'But what is it?'

Haig folded the camp stools and put them back inside the diorama. He methodically rolled one of his queerly shaped cigarettes, lit it and puffed smoke like a fog.

'*Atna-arilta-kuma*,' he said, 'is the rite for Aboriginal girls corresponding to circumcision for youths. The initiates are deflowered with a stone knife, after which, as the textbooks say, the elders performing the ceremony enter into them.'

He blew more smoke.

After a long silence, Corless raised his voice in a startled query. 'Blackmail?'

Haig's face showed signs of strain. 'Suppose,' he said, 'you found yourself involved in a stunt like *atna-arilta-kuma*, you'd hate it to become public, wouldn't you? But it wasn't Laurie Moore who did the blackmailing. Remember what he told the man, Jacks, in Winonga – *I'm on to a filthy game. A game worse than murder.* I'm beginning to think your cousin wasn't a bad type, after all. Somebody made a mistake about him, so he was killed before he could talk. Wild drinking brawlers are often mistaken for something far more poisonous.'

Corless felt tiny dead patches in his jaw muscles and knew them for signs of overtaut nerves. He said, 'What next, Digger?'

Haig did not speak. A bustle among the tourists announced the return of the Dream Time Land magnates. Corless saw Rusking, smiling pleasantly, attended by Julie Flax and Mallet. Close behind them were Mrs Ashwood and Martha Rea.

Rusking clapped his hands for attention. 'Ladies and gentlemen,' he said. 'On to Alchera Four. But again a word of warning. The path is difficult so – watch your guides!'

Haig's hand gripped Corless's shoulder.

'You asked what next,' he said softly. 'Obvious son. We find the place of *atna-arilta-kuma*. But first I've got to make sure that little waitress, Elsie Mannus, doesn't go the way of Laurie Moore.'

CHAPTER 7

Haig went away as the crowd moved out, but Corless stayed where he was. In the middle of a small group displaying no particular hurry was Mrs Ashwood, her eyes glowing, her soft face dreamy, her lovely voice languid.

'We're coming to the interesting part of Dream Time Land,' she told her listeners. 'The part with the real Alchera meaning. I never miss it. Yet it's only a foretaste, after all. Oh, dear, yes. There's one supreme experience granted only to a lucky few. One is taken *into the ground*. One meets the *Iruntarinia*. One has a demonstration of the true magic of life. It's beyond imagination. The sublimity – '

Mrs Ashwood and party went by, leaving Corless in the grip of furious thoughts. The possible leaders in this blackmail *atna-arilta-kuma* were not many – Carl Rusking, Ovid Mallet, Julie Flax, Austin Flax. If Mrs Ashwood also had a part in it, then it seemed to follow inevitably that Martha Rea knew of it. And this, Corless found, was deadly to contemplate.

He was the last to go down to Alchera Four. The path was so narrow and winding that he realised that Rusking had not spoken idly when he warned the tourists to be careful. Somewhere below him were more than a hundred people chattering against the background of a native chant, yet he was cut off as though he were a hundred miles away.

And the loneliness was abruptly accentuated when he heard something move in the jungle on his right. He stopped and the sound stopped. He started again and again he heard the noise. A clipping, scratching noise, not on the ground but among the leaves. He could have sworn someone chuckled hoarsely. He understood now how the black people were able to elevate a powerful belief in malignant, darkness-haunting magic.

His nerves had built up to some really fancy twitching when the plat holding Alchera Four opened out and he saw the familiar orange glow. The chanting ceased, the talking ceased and someone began to address the tourists; not Rusking this time but, to Corless's surprise, Ovid Mallet. And speaking well, too. Maybe it was because you couldn't see Mallet's face where he stood aside from the light and so were not prejudiced by his bitter expression.

'At Alchera Three,' Mallet said, 'we saw how the Aborigine in his myth expresses a universal longing. The instinctive yearning for safety, peace, power, control of fate and environment which we all have. Alchera Four teaches how the blackfellow realised law and how he tried to circumvent it.

'The law is pain – '

In the diorama only a small, yellow, sandy area had been illuminated. Now the light expanded and Apma, snake and man, came into view. The man was upright, and the Snake lifted its head from several great coils so that, side by side, both faced a youth who stood with his back to the tourists. The man and the snake were both etched with lines of suffering, but again the snake's air of knowledge was the dominating feature. Knowledge of life, of power, of pain.

Mallet said, 'Pain is a condition of life. Why this is so, the blackfellow knew no more than we do. But he did know it was inescapable. Therefore, Apma decreed, let us make use of pain; let us impose pain to avoid pain that comes savagely, blindly, out of the unknown, striking without reason. Let us conquer pain by deliberately inuring ourselves to it and making it the condition of gaining the Alchera knowledge, authority, happiness.'

Mallet paused, then continued harshly, 'Let us hurt when it hurts most and so drive the lesson home unforgettably. Therefore Apma the Snake lays down the law that pain is the initiation into manhood. And here one of his sons stands before him being told that the time of trial is upon him. The boy has had a carefree childhood. Now he will learn the reality of life. It will not be a short or easy trial. Years must pass before the requirements of pain are met, but the lad does not know that. If he did he would flee.'

The circumference of light widened to show that several lubras had joined Apma and the youth.

'He is saying goodbye to his mother, sisters and friends. He will come back to them, but he will be another person. In his eyes will be the dark light of secrets no woman may know.'

The scene shifted once more. The youth was seated on the ground and the Snake decorated his body with down glued on with blood. Then a change of light brought a fresh queer scene into view. Several men held the boy above their heads while Apma the Snake lay nearby, watching with avid eyes.

'The first part of the ordeal is mild,' said Mallet. 'The men are throwing the youth in the air and catching him. Up he goes four, five, six times, hurled high by powerful arms. This strange flight serves to disturb his childhood sense of security. Whirling in the air, he finds his world no longer the secure immovable system he thought it was. It also serves to teach him that if he trusts his teachers, just as their strong arms save him from crashing on the ground, so he will come through the long torment of initiation to find himself in lasting spiritual security.'

Mallet touched a button on the switchboard. The light moved over to reveal Apma, man and snake, and two other men taking the youth into a thick grove of trees.

'Here he meets real pain,' said Mallet. 'He is circumcised with a roughly wielded stone knife. He must not cry out for that would show he hasn't the makings of a man and he would be outcast. When the bleeding is staunched, he is left alone in those trees for many days. He is fed with food carried there secretly by old men. He may move around if he wishes, but he must not be seen and so he is given a *namatwinna*, a bull-roarer, a flat piece of wood on the end of a cord which he whirls as he walks, thereby making a loud moaning noise. Back in the camp, the women believe the noise to be made by some great spirit and so they rigidly avoid the place.'

In the darkness behind the diorama arose a rhythmical booming. Almost you could imagine a lost soul moaning over the earth. The noise died and Mallet spoke again.

'When the prescribed time has passed, the Great Snake enters the bush, brings the youth out and shows him briefly to the women. Then begin the preparations for the more dreadful, more agonising rite of sub-incision.'

Nearby, Corless saw Mrs Ashwood busily writing notes on the back of an envelope. He thought, That's the letter I gave her, not opened yet.

He felt a hand on his shoulder and Rusking's voice said quietly, 'What do you think of it, Jock?'

Corless looked at the pleasant youthful face, faintly golden in the diorama light. It was not the kind of face to hide thoughts of *atna-arilta-kuma*, not the face of a human vampire.

He made some commonplace compliments and Rusking smiled. 'Jock,' he said, his hand still pressing the other's shoulder, 'I sometimes think I'm the luckiest man alive. I have an art to practise, a fascinating story to tell and a lesson to teach. As well, I'm making a good living. What more could a man want?' He paused to listen to Mallet, then he went on, 'Ovid's doing a good job, isn't he?'

'How long has he been with you, Carl?'

'He came here three months ago. On a holiday. He says he fell in love with the place. He wants to buy it.'

'Why don't you sell it to him? He's wealthy. He'd pay well.'

'Sell this show?' Rusking was suddenly tense. 'God, no! I made it. It stays mine.'

'What about Austin?'

'He taught me a lot,' Rusking said. 'But I made it. I *created* Dream Time Land. As a matter of fact, Julie means more in the show than Austin. You saw him at Alchera Two. But Julie's an artist.' He stopped, eyed Corless queerly and said, 'Which reminds me, Jock. We've got one fool around here already, that policeman, Bailey.'

'So I'm not to fall for her, eh?' said Corless dryly. 'You've got a claim there, I suppose.'

'No,' said Rusking seriously. 'As far as I'm concerned, Julie can marry who she likes. But the operative word is *likes*. It's hard to explain Julie. She hurts men who don't understand her, though she hurts herself more. I said she's an artist. She's like those drugs that save your life at the right time but will cripple you if taken when you don't need them. I've learnt to know her in three years, Jock.'

Corless thought it was time to change the subject. 'What are the *Iruntarinia*?' he asked.

Rusking gave him a curious glance. '*Iruntarinia*? They're spirits who live in the ground and in rocks. You'll learn about them in later Alchera.'

'Will we be taken *into the ground* in the later Alchera?'

Rusking started. Then he laughed softly. 'You've been listening to Delia Ashwood. She's an enthusiast, that woman. I really believe she lives every part of Dream Time Land in her imagination. This place would be worth a million pounds if everybody was like her. One of these days she'll write a book about it.'

At the diorama, Mallet said, 'More pain, and still more pain. The haven of power and knowledge for the youth can't be seen for the fog of pain. He has recovered from the first trial. The second, more excruciating test is upon him.'

The light shifted. The black youth was being decorated again, watched over by Apma. Always that watching by the Snake as though the scenes were bodied forth from his mind.

Haig's voice said, 'Very good show, Rusking. But why not make it completely realistic?'

The detective's sudden appearance startled Rusking. 'How?' he demanded.

'By showing the equivalent rites for women.'

Rusking said, 'That's not funny, Inspector Haig. Perhaps you don't know that women's initiation rites are pretty horrible. Nothing like them could ever be staged. Or even hinted at. But if they could, it would add nothing to the native myth.'

'They're called *atna-arilta-kuma*, aren't they?' said Haig, his manner idle but his eyes hard.

'That's the title,' Rusking replied evenly.

There was space for several breaths, then Haig said, 'I've been talking to a tourist who's seeing the show for his fifteenth time.'

'That's a compliment to Dream Time Land.'

'Maybe. He says tonight's is the best of the lot, though he prefers to listen to you rather than to Mallet. He says there's more what he calls *feel* in the show tonight, which is interesting.'

'Why?'

'It means,' said Haig slowly, 'that instead of Laurie Moore's death depressing the show as one would expect, it's done the show good – as though a weight has been removed.'

Rusking stiffened. 'That's a damn slur, Haig. But leave my feelings out of it and consider two things. In the first place, the tourists know nothing about Laurie Moore. We've made sure of that. We don't want talk of murder in Dream Time Land, and so far there's none, though some of the tourists are puzzled because the police are here. Second, consider just what is the real show. The dioramas, Haig, and the figures in them. Now tell me just how could anybody's death affect those figures?'

A rude expression seemed to hover on Haig's lips. If so, he ruled it out. 'I've read the blurb on your programmes,' he said. 'It tells about the great artist meeting the great bushman – blah-blah, and how this meeting resulted in Dream Time Land and how Julie inspired you and Austin (though it says nothing of Genghiz Khan) to greater flights of artistry – blah-blah. But it leaves one important question unanswered. Why did you pick on Ungamillia as the place to stage Dream Time Land?'

Rusking gave this some consideration.

'Quite a lot of factors were involved. The price, the scenery, the tourist trade, the jungle – an ideal setting for the show – the lorikeets,' he said. 'But I guess the main reason was that Austin liked the place. There's the name, for instance. Ungamillia – the Evening Star. That caught his fancy.'

Haig nodded. He appeared lost in thought. At the diorama, Mallet was nearing the end of the first great initiatory rites, circumcision and sub-incision. All the spotlights blazed. Every portion of the diorama's composite picture was in view; Apma, man and snake, the youth, the elders, the women. The tourists were very quiet.

'What about blackmail?' asked Haig with brutal suddenness.

Rusking's face sagged into astonishment. 'What do you mean?'

The detective told him of the meaning of Laurie Moore's statement of debts.

'Madness!' cried the artist. Some tourists looked round, and he clamped his voice down to a throbbing murmur. 'There's nothing of the kind here. It's a vile trick. You made this up.'

'What about Mrs Ashwood's supreme experience *in the ground*?' demanded Haig, thereby astonishing Corless. He had not noticed Haig at hand when Mrs Ashwood spoke to her knot of listeners.

'Mrs Ashwood?' said Rusking. 'Jock was talking about her, too. That woman's mad. She lives in fantasy. She's let the atmosphere – '

Without any premonitory sound, a parrot appeared in the diorama. It seemed to Corless that he had never before seen such a gigantic bird.

'That damned cockatoo!' said Rusking and was gone.

Corless realised that he had been deceived again by the perfect perspective and proportions of the diorama; that against the small models Genghiz Khan had a monstrous aspect. He had then the explanation of the queer noises that had accompanied him down the path to Alchera Four – Genghiz Khan making a stealthy approach to the fun and games.

Chuckling evilly, Genghiz Khan elevated his crest and launched a ferocious attack with beak and claw on one of the models of Apma the Snake. Huge rips appeared in Apma's plastic skin. Then Genghiz Khan cocked a cunning eye as Rusking advanced out of the darkness behind him with murderous mien. The cockatoo left his retreat too late. Rusking dived forward, seized him like a football and bore him off to captivity despite his furious resistance.

'Damn you, Austin Flax!' he shrieked without any justification whatsoever.

The tourists cheered. Mallet tried to save the situation by leading them immediately on to Alchera Five, but once more the awesome atmosphere of Dream Time Land had been sabotaged.

Haig said, 'File that under Odd Mysteries, Jock.'

'What on earth for?'

'Why didn't Austin reply, "*And damn you, too*"?'

There was only one reason, of course. Austin had not replied because he was not present. Corless had an onslaught of fear.

'Digger, what about Elsie Mannus?'

'Don't worry,' said Haig. 'There's a copper at the cafe watching her all the time. But I'll have to see about the old man – '

The detective had a word with two constables, who presently departed without any fanfare, then he and Corless joined the procession to Alchera Five where the usual orange glow illuminated a desert scene and the loudspeaker descanted to the glory of Apma the Snake.

> *Over the fires Apma spies;*
> *From the stars Apma peers;*
> *Apma is light and fire and star.*
> *Apma, Oknirrabata! Wei!*

Rusking apparently had disposed of Genghiz Khan, for he appeared beside the diorama, a handkerchief round his left hand marking the consequence of his beak and claw encounter.

'Alchera Five – a climactic,' he announced.

His face was indistinct, but Corless thought that the crisp authority of his voice was frayed, that he was suffering the effect of Haig's *atna-arilta-kuma* bombshell.

He pulled a switch and a subdued light spread over the entire diorama, giving the tourists a thrill of surprise. Alchera Five was the biggest and most spectacular in the series so far. It depicted a night scene. White stars burned in a purple sky over a receding line of fires. In the rectangle round the fires sat rows of Aborigines. On each side of the fires was a file of dancing spearman. Beyond the fires squatted three elders in awe-inspiring head-dresses, the effect of which was augmented with regalias of white down and designs painted in red ochre.

Beyond them again, partly hidden in a bush covert, sat the youth who had been the subject of the initiation ceremonies. Standing over him, but less clearly seen, was Apma the Man. Apma the Snake was absent. At the end nearer the audience was a dancing woman weirdly outlined with white pipeclay.

The correct atmosphere had been rescued and the tourists began to clap.

'Thank you,' said Rusking.

'Damn all women,' said a disgruntled voice behind Corless. He turned to see an elderly irate gentleman.

'What's the trouble?'

'The missus. Told her to stick by me. But did she? No. Standing somewhere in the crowd enjoying the fun while I'm chasing round wondering if she's lost in the damned jungle.'

He moved on, peering into women's faces.

Rusking said, 'Alchera Five is the homecoming of the boy after his first trials of pain. The lubra dancing at this end is his mother, ready to welcome him. You see Apma the Man just behind the boy. Because this is, so to speak, a public ceremony, having lubras present, Apma the Snake is not apparent. But he is present. You may see him among the stars.'

In the stars of the diorama's sky, the dark patches formed the silhouette of a snake's body just above the boy waiting in the covert. Corless did not know if Rusking manipulated a switch, but suddenly he perceived the Snake's eyes, sage and potent as they had been when glowing up through the water in Alchera One. The great body and gleaming eyes, suspended in the artificial sky, gave a strange impression of omniscience and authority and fate.

'When you leave Dream Time Land tonight,' Rusking continued, 'look up into the sky and, if it is clear, you will see Apma among the real stars, in the dark patches of the Milky Way. For some tribes, the figure formed by those black spaces is *Erlia* the Great Emu ancestor, but we are with the Snake totem and so it is Apma we see.'

There was more applause.

Rusking bowed.

'The boy,' he said, 'comes to his mother for a respite. He is still her son, but he has gone beyond her. He is no longer a happy-go-lucky piccaninny but a man. He has learnt strange secrets which she will never know. There are more secrets to come, but he has learnt his place in the tribe, in history, in destiny. He knows now, though dimly, he is that Snake in the sky above him, he is all snakes in the bush, he is the scores of memorials to his great ancestor and that all of them are him.'

'He is near the great awakening,' a woman whispered.

It was Mrs Ashwood. Someone else spoke, and Corless looked round. The elderly tourist had apparently found his wife, for he was berating the woman with him. 'A fair thing's a fair thing, Madge. I thought the infernal blacks had got you.'

They passed on.

'This is the last time,' said Rusking, 'that the youth's mother will appear in a ceremony with him – unless he happens to die before she does. *Then* she would take part in his funeral rites. So, when he leaves that cover to dance along the fires, she will embrace him, but the embrace will be a surrender. He is coming back to her, but really he has gone away for ever.'

Rusking paused and a man asked a question.

'Mr Rusking, in everything we have seen so far, the subject has been a youth. Are there similar ceremonies for a girl? That is, do native girls go through initiations like the boys?'

It wasn't Haig's voice, but Corless was prepared to bet that Haig had inspired the question. He could not see the detective, though he saw Sergeant Clough's burly form near where the question came from.

Rusking was worried.

'Girls do undergo rites, both physical and symbolic,' he said hesitantly.

'Any particular reason why you don't illustrate those ceremonies?'

'Now, look here,' began Rusking warmly. Then he switched to another tack and managed a wry smile. 'There's a very good reason for not illustrating the ceremonies,' he said. 'The heavens mightn't fall on me, but the police most certainly would.'

'Can you give us any idea what the ceremonies are?'

Rusking tried hard to pinpoint the persistent enquirer.

'I could,' he said, eyeing the tourists where the questions originated. 'But I won't. It's a subject for anthropologists only.'

'Lucky anthropologists,' said the voice.

There was a laugh that shrivelled into a gasp. The eyes of the shadowy snake in the sky seemed to move. By heaven! thought Corless, they *are* moving. They came forward almost imperceptibly. Just as gradually there formed round them a scarcely visible face. A great body took shape under the face until there came into view a giant whose head touched the stars; a giant only – Corless understood in a flash – because of comparison with the tiny figures in the diorama.

Then his heart began to pound. It was the black face that had stared at him from the jungle soon after his arrival. He looked at Rusking and was aware of another shock. If the artist's slack jaw and bulging eyes were an indication, Rusking was just as surprised as his audience.

The black figure approached until it straddled the line of fires. Someone shouted, 'Bucktooth Tommy!' The huge black retreated quickly. A man brushed past Corless and pushed into the jungle beside the diorama. Haig for a certainty, said Corless to himself. The form of the black visitant vanished into the dark shadows behind the diorama.

Rusking still stared. Then Mallet joggled his elbow and whispered to him. He straightened up, faced the puzzled tourists and showed a smile.

'Ladies and gentlemen,' he said. 'Always the Fire Dance ceremony is ended with a display of magic. You have just seen the magic. And now' – he glanced at his wrist-watch – 'because we're running behind schedule, we'll take our second intermission now instead of waiting till after Alchera Six. Thank you, ladies and gentlemen.'

On emerging from Dream Time Land, Corless had a feeling of incongruity. The westering sun set slow-moving cumulus clouds on fire, poured a lambent haze into the Winonga valley, outlined the big house with gold. To maintain the effect, he thought, you should come out of Dream Time Land into a black night.

He watched the tourists straggling across the garden towards the cafe. He saw Mrs Ashwood and Martha Rea go to the house, followed by Rusking and Julie, with Mallet plodding behind them. In this quiet evening scene, there was no hint of murder or blackmail.

Hearing his name called, he turned to see Haig leaving the *mia-mia* entrance. Haig moved unhurriedly, but Corless had the impression his mild demeanour masked a tumultuous anger.

'Well?'

The ridges of flesh above Haig's mouth quivered.

'Not well, Jock. I think I know *who* and *what*, but I don't know *how* and *where*.' He rolled one of his thick cigarettes. 'Who shouted "*Bucktooth Tommy*"?'

'Old Austin – I *think*. I didn't see him.'

'I reckoned it was Austin, too.' Haig got his cigarette burning. 'I went into the bush after the black, but I had no hope. The scrub's too thick and he was gone before I went ten yards. He was the feller you saw earlier?'

'Yes. And that raises a large question. Why is he showing himself?'

Haig gazed thoughtfully down into the golden light of Winonga valley.

'File him under Greek Gifts,' he said. 'He's not the only Greek gift today, but it's taken me too long to realise it. The way Laurie Moore was disposed of was the first. Yair, a Greek gift.' He pondered again and added inconsequentially, 'Rusking's an actor as well as an artist.'

'Yet I'll take my oath the black was a surprise to him,' said Corless. 'Though he reacted quickly when Mallet nudged him.'

'Yes, passed the black off as a display of magic,' growled the detective. 'Well, that's all right with me. I don't blame him for trying to stop the tourists from guessing something's wrong. But announcing the second interval because they were running late is another matter. Running late me fat aunt's pet billy-goat! Where are they all now?'

'In the house. I saw them go in – all except Austin. Of course, he could be there, too.'

'And all talking of *atna-arilta-kuma*,' said Haig. 'That's why Rusking brought on the interval. They're in there, tongues hammering. "*This damned Haig, he's on to us. What the hell are we going to do? Or maybe just the opposite. What the devil is this business Haig threw at me? Atna-arilta-kuma? Blackmail? You people know what he meant? What is going on here?*" Which do you back, Jock?'

'How would I know?'

'I bet your Nightingale could tell us.'

'Digger, she's not – '

'Let it ride,' said Haig. 'And let 'em talk. I'm hungry.'

He turned and made leisurely for the cafe. Then he suddenly changed direction and headed for the rear of the house. A policeman leaning casually against the garage wall straightened up.

Haig barked, 'What's the idea, Forrest? I thought I told you to watch the Mannus girl?'

The constable, a slow-talking type, pointed at the kitchen window. A large window, affording a clear view of the interior, it also afforded a view of Elsie Mannus busy at an electric range.

'The girls at the cafe take turns in the house,' the policeman said. 'It's Elsie Mannus's turn tonight.'

Haig glowered for a while. Presently he said, 'Okay. Just don't let her get away from you, that's all. Come on, Jock.'

The cafe was full, and the waitresses were busy, but Haig waylaid one who led them to a corner table and took their order.

When she had gone, Haig said, 'Did you see where everybody was during the ruction?'

'I'm not sure of everybody,' said Corless, thinking back. 'Rusking and Mallet were in plain view all the time – at least, I'm certain about Rusking for he was speaking, and almost certain about Mallet. Martha Rea and Mrs Ashwood were on my left, and I'll swear they didn't move. But I'm afraid I'm not sure of Julie. It's my impression she was in her usual place on the far side of the diorama. Austin I didn't see at all.'

'Well, the black could be a black unless Austin – ' Haig let the sentence die. 'Where did the yell come from?' he asked.

'Somewhere behind me.'

The waitress arrived with steak and eggs for Haig and cold meat and salad for Corless. Haig looked up at her. She was a bouncy blue-eyed girl who bore his scrutiny with professional equanimity.

'Is your name Kathy Winn?'

'It is, Mr Haig,' she said pertly. 'And if you want to know where old Austin was at lunch-time, I can tell you. He was here.'

Haig leaned back slowly.

'Now this is service. How would you know I'd be asking about Austin's whereabouts?'

'He told me you would.'

'Sounds like collaboration,' said Haig.

'It's saving time and fuss.' Kathy Winn straightened the tablecloth. 'There'll be no check for you, gentlemen. You're guests of Ungamillia.'

She went away.

'What I like about this place,' said Haig, getting to work on his steak and eggs, 'is the beautiful manner in which everybody knows what's going on – '

Fifteen minutes later, they left the cafe and set off for the house, walking into the after-light of sunset. They took the path to the front of the house, turned the corner and stopped. About twenty feet from the hole he had filled in earlier, old Austin was down to his knees in another hole, digging industriously. As he swung the pick, sweat spattered from his face and he half sang, half hummed his mangled version of 'Onward Christian Soldiers'. Genghiz Khan strutted nearby at the end of a chain.

Haig walked forward, tapped Austin on the shoulder and pointed at the cockatoo.

'The last time I saw this brute,' he said, 'he'd just been arrested by Brother Rusking for desecrating Alchera Four. How did you reclaim him?'

'Heard him squawk,' said Austin, wiping sweat out of his eyes. 'Went down to the gate an' met Carl there an' took Genghiz over. Brought him back here an', if you want proof, there was a couple of Johns pokin' round.'

'I sent them,' said Haig sardonically. 'They told me you were here. But, old party, you didn't stay here.'

Austin climbed out of the hole and investigated an itch under his shirt collar.

'I went down to Alchera Five,' he mumbled, 'after peggin' Genghiz out.'

'In time to see a strange black?'

'Yair.'

'And then?'

'Come back here, had a bit o' tea an' started on the hole again.'

Haig tugged gently at Austin's open waistcoat. 'You didn't by any means *know* you would see the black?'

'Gawd, no!' Austin dropped into the hole and sat on the edge. He took out his pipe and began to fill it with fingers that showed just the slightest tremble.

'You told us Bucktooth was dead,' said Haig. 'Died fifteen years ago in Alice Springs, so why yell his name?'

'Silly mistake,' muttered Austin. 'Got a shock. First glance the feller looked like Bucktooth, an' I got excited, I s'pose. Stupid thing to do.'

'Who was the black?'

Austin shook his head energetically. 'Dunno. Somebody playin' tricks, but I don't know who.'

Haig squatted down on one heel, cupped his chin in his hand and rested his elbow on his knee.

'Old party,' he said, 'you're getting desperate. Usually you're down in Dream Time Land, not missing a moment of it, hoping all the time to get the chance of getting a big laugh by giving *your* idea of the myths. Today, however, you tear yourself away, digging your holes, and sneaking back to Dream Time Land every now and then because you know something's badly wrong. But you've got to keep on digging before it's too late.'

Austin put a match to his pipe and his blue eyes held a fierce glint.

'There's gold here, an' I'm goin' to find it if I got to dig up every foot of the hill.'

'That,' said Haig, 'is something you can keep for the fairies. *Or* the *Iruntarinia*.'

Austin waved his pipe and began to adduce reasons for his belief in gold at Ungamillia. Corless forgot to listen. Genghiz Khan, eyeing Haig with intense curiosity, waddled towards him, moving – Corless was enchanted to see – so delicately his chain made no noise. His black shiny eye was fixed intently on the tight part of Haig's trousers bulging out over the supporting heel. His big curved beak opened. Corless held his breath. When that beak nipped through the trousers, Haig would break the world record for the sitting high jump.

But such joy was not to be. At the crucial moment, Haig's hand swooped round, seized Genghiz Khan and hurled him away. The cockatoo vented his rage in wild screams. Then with his usual disregard of justice he said, 'Damn you, Austin Flax!'

'An' damn you, too,' said the old man absentmindedly.

'I think,' said Haig, 'the cocky may have something, old party.'

Austin stood up and Haig stood up with him.

'What do you mean?' the old man demanded angrily.

'The bird said, "Damn you!" and so do I. You're not digging for gold.'

'Then what am I diggin' for?'

Haig became silkily dangerous. 'All your holes are close to the house, which makes a man wonder if you're looking for a kind of secret cellar, say, where people can go *into the ground* and practise something like *atna-arilta-kuma*.'

Austin abruptly sat down again in the hole and put his head between his hands.

Haig said, 'You know what *atna-arilta-kuma* is?'

The old man nodded. 'Yair. Nearly got killed for it once.'

'You what!' ejaculated the staggered detective.

Austin gave a quick bird-like glance round, as though making sure he could not be overheard.

'One time,' he said in a lowered tone, 'I was out in the Hartz Ranges. I heard an *atna-arilta-kuma* was due, an' I set out to watch it. A risky game, because it's secret, see. Only three, four old men of the tribe are let in on the woman-makin' ceremony. I had a bit o' trouble findin' out where it was goin' to happen, but I got it out of a young buck who was jealous of the old men. You see, Digger Haig, when you look into it, all the Aboriginal customs is fixed for the old men to get the best of things. Best food, best lubras, best treatment, everybody jumpin' when the old man talks. Everythin's made for the old men like this *atna* business. Anyway, I got on the scene – well hidden, I reckoned. But they smelt me out, an' I had to cut an' run. Got away with a spear stuck in me arm. Never went back there for fifteen year when all them old men was dead. If they'd had their way, I'd been dead, too.'

'Laurie Moore's dead,' said Haig.

Austin caught the implication.

'Gawd's truth!' he cried. 'I tell y' there's nothin' like that here. Impossible!'

Up under the portico someone moved. The daylight had faded, but they could see Julie against the light in the hall.

'So there you are,' she said. 'I've been wondering where you two got to. Come on in.'

Corless and Haig mounted the steps, and Julie led them into the hall among the array of spears and waddies and death bones and other Aboriginal paraphernalia. She had changed into an apricot-pink gown which was purely feminine and decorative. She was all grace and fire and subtly pervading perfume. Her eyes were a very dark purple.

She looked at them, and her smile faltered. 'Don't be hard on Austin, Mr Haig,' she said. 'He's harmless.'

'No one's harmless round here,' snapped Haig. 'And that goes for you, too.'

Her smile grew wide and uninhibited. 'Yes, I'm a danger-ous woman. But there is no *atna-arilta-kuma* at Ungamillia, Mr Haig. We're not an *abominable* family.'

'So Rusking's done his duty,' Haig growled.

The girl regarded him thoughtfully. 'If I make the correct inference,' she said, 'you intended Carl to tell us Laurie's list of debts was really a message about blackmail.'

'You make the correct inference,' said Haig. 'He has told you. What's the result?'

'Good heavens, Mr Haig! There's only one result. If anybody here is guilty of blackmail, do you think they'd say so?' Julie's impatience was only momentary. 'You're not making this message up,' she asked gravely.

'I am not.'

'Then Laurie must have. I can't understand why.'

'But Laurie Moore is dead.'

Julie said, 'Yes, yes. But why, Mr Haig? If there's mystery here, it has come from outside.'

'I'll remind you of the black at the Fire Dance,' said Haig brusquely.

'That?' She played see-saws with her interlaced fingers. 'There you have the only tangible mystery. Nobody here knows who or what he is or where he came from. Someone playing a joke, Mr Haig, or else he's your murderer.'

'You don't know which?'

Her laugh held exasperation.

'Must you suspect everything we say? Mr Haig, the solution is simple. You've got a number of police here. Get them to search Ungamillia from top to bottom. Search Dream Time Land from end to end. Do that and perhaps you'll be satisfied.' She laughed again wryly. 'Oh, let's give over talking. Come and have dinner. You'll be better after you've had something to eat.'

But Haig, in no mood to be better, said that he and Corless had already eaten at the cafe. What they wanted now was to examine Laurie Moore's room without interruption.

Showing no reaction to the rebuff, Julie said, 'I'll take you upstairs.'

As they moved towards the staircase, Corless glanced through the doorway into the dining-room and had a glimpse of Martha Rea leaning back in her chair and laughing. The clean line of her throat rising from a white dress, her hair waving back, the white gleam of her teeth, made him savage. All he need do to stop that laugh was stand in the doorway. Then she would become as hard and stony as pre-Cambrian rock. But fair was fair. She had the same effect upon him.

Going up the stairs, he thought of several new maledictions he could teach Genghiz Khan.

The landing opened into a panelled corridor which ran the width of the house. Julie turned to the right and stopped at the first door on the left.

'Your room, Mr Haig. Right opposite you is a spare. Next to that is Laurie's.'

'Thank you,' said Haig.

'This is yours, Jock,' said Julie, moving to the room beside Haig's. She opened the door, switched on the light and touched his arm in a friendly gesture. 'Your ports are here. I had them brought up. I do hope you are comfortable.'

'Thank you, Julie.'

She looked at him, and her eyes were warm.

'Jock, this was Laurie's home. I want you to feel it is your home, too.'

'That's very nice of you,' he said.

She smiled and returned to the landing, slim, elegant, no back-swagger or hip-wobble. He thought she moved very gracefully.

Going into his room, he eyed his bags alongside the bed, then he opened the french windows and stepped out on to the balcony. This, he saw, extended past Haig's windows. Farther on, beyond the portico, a similar balcony jutted out. He remembered that he had seen Mrs Ashwood peering from that balcony. He guessed that if Mrs Ashwood was there, Martha Rea's room was almost certain to be next door.

He turned back into the room in time to see Haig coming in. The detective's ill-humour had left him. A light burned inside him. He was alive and quick and vital.

'Right-oh, Jock. To work, son.'

Out in the corridor, they went to the room which Julie said had been Laurie's and opened the door. Haig switched on the light.

Corless looked at the untidy array of clothes hanging over chairs, at the shoes on the floor, at piles of magazines in the corners, and knew it was Laurie's room without any doubt. It was like Laurie's life, disorderly and unorganised.

Haig said, 'I guess someone's been through the place already, but we'll do it again.'

Five minutes later, he shook his head. The only result of their work was thirty-three pounds and some odd shillings which they had rescued out of various pockets.

'A peculiar bird, your cousin,' said Haig.

He went to the windows and opened them on to a balcony similar to those in the front of the house. By now darkness had fallen. Over on their left glowed the cheerful lights of the cafe, from which issued a cheerful babble. To the right, the lights of the *mia-mia* entrance to Dream Time Land showed above the outbuildings. Beyond them was the black jungle. Below, light from the kitchen window faintly illumined the kitchen porch.

Haig studied this last with some interest. 'I wonder if Moore was given this room or asked for it,' he said. 'It's just a step from here to the top of the porch and from there to the ground is simple. He had an easy way out and in at dead of night. And used it, no doubt.'

Corless had no doubt, either.

Someone turned the porch light on, and Haig swore softly. The new light brought the garage into view, and they could now see Constable Forrest, the policeman watching over Elsie Mannus. Constable Forrest had a cup of tea in one hand and a meat pie in the other, and his jaws were in action.

'That's torn it,' said Haig, muting his fury to a whisper. 'Come back inside.'

He shut the windows and drew the curtains.

Corless said, 'Anything wrong with a man eating a meat pie?'

'Hell, no,' gritted Haig. He did a quarter-deck march across the room, kicking Laurie Moore's shoes out of the way.

'Well, why blow your top?'

'I'm not worried about Forrest,' said Haig, marching and counter-marching. 'It's Constable Riley I'm thinking of.'

'Riley?'

Haig halted in front of Corless and wagged his forefinger. 'Jock, so far I've avoided doing the obvious thing, which is to line everybody up in the lounge downstairs and put 'em through the usual grill. I don't want to do that. Where would it get me? Julie told you. If they're guilty they won't own up, and nothing could make 'em own up. But I threw the bomb about the *atna-arilta-kuma* business at Rusking and left them alone. What they don't know is that Riley is planted under the shrubbery by the dining-room windows. *Now* do you see why it twisted my tail to find Forrest eating his head off out there?'

'Not quite.'

'Dammit, if they spot a policeman obviously watching the house, are they going to risk being overheard? If there's one policeman, there could be another. The pie and tea show they *have* spotted Forrest. Not his fault, but the play's spoilt. Anyway, we'll let Riley stay put. He *might* hear something.'

'I see,' said Corless.

'You don't see at all.' Haig pushed the clothes off a chair, sat down and rolled a cumbersome cigarette. 'What's the oddest thing about this business so far, Jock?'

'I can think of twenty odd things,' said Corless.

'The oddest,' said Haig, blowing a smudge of smoke. 'I mentioned Greek gifts. Why was Moore's body tossed in front of the car at the Well of St Giles?'

'Obviously to make his death look like an accident.'

'Ah!' said Haig, his eyes and mouth opened triumphantly so that he looked more like a gargoyle than ever. 'That's what we were intended to think. I don't mean we were meant to think his death was an accident – though that would have helped – but we were intended to realise it was an attempt to make us think it. It's a beautiful sample of someone trying too hard.'

'What in thunder are you getting at?' said the bemused Corless.

'Some years ago,' said Haig soberly, 'I was arresting a lout and I took the most gorgeous kick in the groin you've ever had. I went to the quack, and he kept me under observation. But what the devil do you think he observed? My left knee! I thought the coot was mad, but he was right. In the groin I had a bruise that came to nothing, but on the left knee there grew a carbuncle like a volcano, and I had seventeen of the cows before the doc's serum cleaned 'em up.

'The Well of St Giles is the groin. But where is the real infection? Not being doctors, we'd have gone off chasing Laurie Moore's back trail and got nowhere. The whole idea of Laurie's being killed how and where he was killed was to take our minds right away from the real problem. Supposing you'd wanted to kill him, what would you have done? Remember we're in the hills.'

'I guess,' said Corless slowly, 'I'd have dumped him in some deep tangle of scrub hard to get at. Say, one of the gorges.'

'Exactly.' Haig looked at his cigarette, discovered it was out and threw it away. 'You'd merely have made him disappear. But someone was afraid of doing that. They thought that if Laurie'd disappeared we'd start looking for him and so light on something – not Laurie Moore – they'd hate like hell to see brought out.

'So Laurie is killed and thrown in front of the car, and we come on the scene and would have gone off on the intended trail but for one thing – Laurie's list of debts. We've got other sore spots that could develop into interesting carbuncles; Mallet and the photograph you said he has – '

'He has it all right,' said Corless heatedly. 'Or he had.'

Haig held up a restraining hand. 'Okay. There's Mallet and his photograph and the signpost he altered; there's a feathered death bone; there's the Ashwood woman and her supreme experience; there's Elsie Mannus and there's old Austin and his holes. Yair' – he was silent for a few seconds – 'and there's a snake that's the nearest approach to infernal wisdom I've ever seen. But I'm not going to wallow in examinations and cross-examinations, alibis and excuses and explanations. There is only one thing that counts – the place where they practise something like *atna-arilta-kuma* to trick people into situations which make them ripe for blackmail. We find that place and we – '

He stopped. The light had gone out.

CHAPTER 8

With his hand pressing hard on Corless's shoulder, Haig whispered, 'Start crawling, Jock, Keep close to me. Remember somebody threw a dart at you.'

There was an unpleasant ten seconds which seemed like an hour as Corless crept on hands and knees over the carpet with his face against Haig's heels, and then the door was open and, lying prone, they looked out into the darkness of the corridor.

Distant sounds penetrated from outside; laughter, talk, the noise of tourists making back to Dream Time Land, but the house was black and formless and still. They could have been alone in the house except for whoever had turned the lights off. Unless, of course, the failure of the lights was due to accident. The tightness of Corless's nerves began to relax.

Then he stiffened as though a thumb had been jabbed on a paralysing plexus. There *was* a light in the house, a shifting glow that came apparently from an open door beyond the landing.

The glow vanished. The darkness intensified. Time had a feeling of thudding to a standstill. Then it speeded into a stampede. The light reappeared and Haig was urging Corless along the corridor on hands and knees.

They went past the landing, slowing down until they merely inched forward. And then they were peering through the doorway from which the light escaped. They saw a torch and a dark figure holding it. The intruder, turned side-on to them, seemed to be occupied in searching through the drawers of a dressing-table.

A minute elapsed and a strange thing happened. The torch was elevated somewhat so that it shone into the mirror above the dressing-table. From the mirror came a reflected beam to illuminate the black face behind the torch. Though it could be seen in profile only, Corless knew it was the face that had peered at him near the cliff-edge, the face they had seen at the Fire Dance Alchera.

'Now!' said Haig and projected himself through the doorway in a tigerish tackle. To Corless, plunging in behind him, it seemed that the floor turned turtle and flung them headlong. He found himself on top of the swearing inspector, wondering how in heck he had arrived in such an absurd position.

'Get off, for hell's sake!' Haig bellowed. Corless rolled clear and they scrambled to their feet. Haig flashed his torch. Except for themselves, the room was empty, and the detective hurried out to the balcony seconds too late. His light touched for a moment a dark figure running across the garden and then it was gone.

'Damn!' he said savagely. He returned into the room and shone the torch on a small stool overturned in the doorway and swore again.

'The oldest trick in the world!' he snarled. 'File yourself under Goats I've Lived With, Haig.'

Corless, sitting on the bed to nurse a painful shin, became aware of a familiar perfume.

'What would the brute be doing in *this* room?' he asked.

'Whose room is it?'

'Martha Rea's.'

Haig, who had been vainly trying the light switch, sniffed the air and laughed sourly.

'The acute senses of the ardent romantic,' he said.

'You go to – '

Corless stopped and thought, What's the use? It made no difference, protesting, and Haig had to be Haig.

'Let's see what the brute was doing,' said Haig.

He stamped over to the dressing-table, directed his torch into various drawers and had a find, a post-card sized photograph partly hidden under a pile of handkerchiefs.

'Look at this, Jock,' he said, in a curiously restrained voice.

The photograph showed in heavily accentuated black and white two naked Aborigines in a small, jungle-walled glade. Corless took one look at the obscene thing and felt sick, but Haig studied it in a cold clinical manner.

'Two facts are evident,' he said. 'This is a picture of part of a vengeance ceremony called the *thumie*. It's the way natives imbue each other with strength when they've got to run and fight hard. Perfectly normal to them.'

'The second thing?'

'The photograph was taken with infra-red film,' said Haig. 'Look at the tremendous detail, the black outlines and the lack of gradations of shading you get in ordinary photographs. But the point about infra-red film, Jock, is that photographs can be taken without the subject being aware of it.'

But Corless was not paying attention. He had conquered his initial revulsion and was studying the photograph carefully, especially a big sloping black shape that formed a part of the right background. He had seen something like this before.

'Mallet,' he said.

'What's that?'

'The same background as in Mallet's photograph.' Corless was excited now.

'You're sure?'

'Absolutely,' said Corless. 'And there's something else, too.'

He described the encounter he'd had with Mallet over the mail delivery and the overlooked letter he had delivered personally to Mrs Ashwood; the letter, addressed in purple print, which he felt sure enclosed a photograph.

'Something to remember,' said Haig. He gazed soberly at the photograph in his hand. 'This is Martha Rea's bedroom!'

'Digger, I'll take my oath – '

'Yes, I know,' said Haig wearily. 'Martha Rea doesn't know about this putrid object. You hate her, she hates you, but you're perfectly sure she wouldn't descend to this. Jock, she either knows about it or she doesn't. In either case, it's a Greek gift and we were meant to find it. So don't let's waste any more time arguing.'

They went downstairs to discover that the cause of the light failure was no accident. The main switch, which they located after some trouble in the kitchen porch, had been pushed to the *off* position. When Haig pulled it to *on*, a dozen lights started burning in the house.

They then investigated the shrubbery under the dining-room windows. Constable Riley was still ensconced. Haig tore gory strips off him concerning the value of crouching outside a silent house without trying to find out why the lights played strange tricks.

'What the hell do you think you are?' the detective roared. 'A poor bloody Roman sentry at Pompeii, eh? Get back to the show and see if the sergeant's got a job you *can* do.'

They caught up to the tourists just as the tail of the procession was entering Alchera Six. All the preceding Alcheras had been lighted up, enabling them to look into each diorama for some large solid object which could have been the background of the photograph. But no such object could be seen.

Nor was there anything of the kind at Alchera Six. It was the usual large, jungle-rimmed, tree-canopied plat with the diorama in a grotto on the west side. Again, a Central Australian scene was depicted; yellow land, red-and-brown, flat-topped ranges with precipitous buttressed slopes, white-trunked ghost gums and clusters of red, blistered boulders.

In the immediate foreground were several elders in weird head-dresses, the youth undergoing initiation –

showing new scars and pipe-clay lines on his body – and Apma, the Man and Snake. The loudspeaker broadcast a softly-sung chant.

> *We approach the cave,*
> *The cave Apma made.*
> *Silence dwells in the cave.*
> *Apma is the cave.*
> *Apma, Oknirrabata! Wei!*

Corless looked at the Snake and the spell was back upon him, the illusion that this was not make-believe for entertainment but an upsurge of *Alcheringa* magic. And the voice that spoke beside him seemed part of the illusion.

'There *is* a great snake loose, Mr Corless.'

He looked at Mrs Ashwood indifferently. Then he looked again with his heart in his mouth. A vast frightening change had come over Mrs Ashwood. The languorous manner, the dream-drugged eyes, the rich rapt voice were gone. Instead Mrs Ashwood was a woman who had taken a fearful shock. She had aged. Her face seemed to have shrunk. Her hands holding the ends of a scarf were knotted hard.

'Are you ill?' he asked.

'I said there was a great snake loose.' Her eyes were unwinking. 'Perhaps you know the snake.'

'I don't understand you,' said Corless.

'Perhaps you don't,' said Mrs Ashwood. 'Perhaps you do. If you do, you'd be better off dead – '

Her glance deflected from him, then she twisted away into the crowd.

Thoroughly disturbed, Corless turned round to see Haig and the Winonga sergeant close behind him.

'There's one of them,' said Haig, nodding towards where Mrs Ashwood had disappeared. 'What about the others?'

'I've had them in sight nearly all the time,' said Sergeant Clough. 'Most of them, that is. It's not easy with a mob like this stringing along the paths. But I saw most of them. Old

Austin, Rusking, Mallet, the Ashwood woman and the nurse, Rea. Only one I'm not sure of is Julie Flax.'

Corless could see Julie in her position beside the diorama. She still wore the gown she was wearing up at the house; not the dress to be traipsing through Dream Time Land in. The pink colour was now a rusty brown in the orange glow from the diorama.

'I can answer for Julie,' said another voice. 'I was with her from the time she left the house till we arrived here.'

Constable Bailey, his face dim under his big hat, had approached unnoticed.

Haig muttered disparagingly about love-sick puppies. Where's Austin now?' he asked.

'Sitting on a log on the other side of the crowd,' said the sergeant. 'Of course, there was an awkward break when the lights went out.'

'When what lights went out?' demanded Haig.

'These lights. The Dream Time lights, from the gate down to here.'

'How long were they out?'

'About a minute, don't you think?' The sergeant appealed to Constable Bailey.

'No more than a minute,' Constable Bailey said.

'How did they go out?' rasped Haig. 'Somebody put them out or what?'

'Nobody knows.' The sergeant scratched his chin. 'There was a lot of confusion. They went out and they came on. The main switch is in that *mia-mia* place. But it was very dark, and there was a lot of confusion as I said, and nobody stepped forward to say they put the lights out or put them on.'

Haig withdrew into a tense, formidable silence. Sergeant Clough eyed him carefully, then he nodded to Bailey, and they moved discreetly away before the storm could break.

'Alchera Six,' announced Rusking from the diorama, and it was a tribute to the atmosphere that everywhere in the circle of tourists cigarettes were dropped and ground out. 'We continue the story of the Snake's son's journey into manhood. He has learnt much, but there is much more awaiting him, and now he is about to make his first visit to a place of tremendous importance and secrecy. Only on rare occasions will he see this place again, such as when, as a fully initiated elder, he himself will induct a young man into the secrets of his race.

'The place is the Snake's *tjurunga* or *churinga* cave. In this cave are kept holy relics of the Snake. They are more than relics. They are the Snake himself, just as all the other memorials we have seen are the Snake and vital with his spirit.

'Here, the elders are chanting stories of Apma. The youth listens carefully. He hears these chants once only, but he must memorise them. If he fails to do so, he may have to wait years before he hears them again. But the chants are mere preliminaries to further trials of his fortitude.'

Another spotlight was switched on, banishing part of the darkness in the diorama to reveal the elders kneeling round the youth and biting his scalp.

'More pain. They bite through hair and flesh. Their teeth crunch against the bones of the skull. They tear huge gaps. The blood flows, spurts. The youth stiffens with the agony, but he stays silent. If he cries out, he is unworthy and his initiation ends there and then. But he does not cry out. He passes the test and is ready for the next.'

Another change of lighting. The elders were about the youth again. Two held his right arm, a third flourished a sharp shining sliver of bone. Apma, Man and Snake, still watched from the rear.

'This, if possible, is a more excruciating trial,' said Rusking. 'The bone is driven slowly under the boy's thumbnail. When the nail lifts, the elder pinches it between his thumb and the bone and tears it away. The other thumbnail is treated similarly.'

A gasp came from the tourists, now completely under Rusking's sway. No, thought Corless, eyeing the Snake; under Apma's sway.

'Great tears pour from the boy's eyes. His body writhes. But he will not cry. He defeats human pain by suffering it voluntarily, rendering himself free for the tremendous life secrets that will follow, and also inuring himself that he will not be borne under when other pain comes.

'While his thumbs bleed, the elders bring a *pitchi*, a wooden vessel, and catch the blood. Blood is the life. They all drink from the *pitchi*, including the boy, and the ceremony is complete. When the boy's thumbs heal, the nails will be puckered, an outward sign that he has not failed in courage and endurance and is ready for the secrets of the cave.'

Behind Rusking, Mallet touched a switch, bringing into view a stark brown hill, boulder-strewn and forbidding. Dark figures, following the Snake, could be seen toiling up a winding path.

'As they go up,' said Rusking, 'the elders are throwing twigs and leaves to the left and right of the path as a warning to Apma's spirit that they are coming. It could be fatal to appear unannounced in the Great Ancestor's presence. At the same time, the elders are singing chants which the boy must memorise, telling how Apma awoke in the Dream Time, how he formed the country, how he established the cave, how he set down tribal laws that will continue to the end of time without change or innovation.

'You cannot see the cave until the elders roll away the slabs of rock, protecting it against prying eyes. They take the youth into it and show him the *tjurunga*, the flat stones inscribed with secret symbols and polished smooth by the rubbing of hundreds of hands. There is the fist *tjurunga*, that of the Great Ancestor himself, and the *tjurunga* of all the boy's intermediate ancestors, all of course one *tjurunga* because all ancestors are the one ancestor. And this explains the paradox which you may have noticed. We started off by saying that this boy was Apma's son, therefore you ask how could he have any intermediate ancestors? The answer is that he not only is Apma's son, he is also the son of everyone of Apma's descendants as well as being Apma himself.

'The elders rub the stones fondly with their hands and then rub them on their stomachs, for the *tjurunga* pulsate with Apma's magic life and rubbing imparts this life to them. Then they show the youth a new stone – his own. It is inscribed with his own secret name, the name he hears for the first time today, the name he will only think about but never utter. They rub him with the stone, then, while one elder holds him firmly from the rear, another takes the stone and strikes him heavily in the stomach with it. Again more pain – this time the pain of victory.

'But the sun is setting. They hasten out of the cave and replace the slabs over the entrance. Because they must be clear of the sacred mountain by nightfall, they hurry down the slope. But they will not sleep this night. Sitting round a little fire, they pass the night chanting the story of Apma, the great, the wise, the powerful, the magical.'

'I, too, want a story chanted,' Haig said softly to Corless. 'Back here, Jock.'

They retreated quietly to where two people waited on the dark side of the glade, a man and a woman. The man was Sergeant Clough. The woman – Corless peered through the gloom – was Martha Rea.

She was indignant. 'Inspector Haig,' she said, 'you're behaving stupidly. These mysterious touches on the shoulder, this being pulled away from my friends for dark conferences! You're play-acting, Mr Haig. What do you want this time?'

'Now, young woman,' said the sergeant heavily. 'This is no time for tantrums.'

'I'm not in a tantrum,' said Martha. 'I want to be treated with commonsense.'

Haig said, 'You interested in photography, Florence?'

'Now what?' cried Martha, but Corless thought he detected a shaky undertone in her voice.

'You heard the question,' said Haig.

'All right,' said Martha. 'If you mean am I an amateur photographer, then no. But what on earth – '

'Well, do you collect what we might call unusual photographs?'

'I don't collect photographs at all,' Martha retorted angrily. 'I have a snap or two of friends or members of my family. But there's nothing unusual – ' She stopped and leaned forward to look at the detective. 'What *are* you after?'

'What did they have to say to you at dinner about *atna-arilta-kuma*?'

'Good gracious! What's that?'

'I want you to tell me.'

'I don't know what you're talking about,' said Martha.

'*Wei! Wei! Wei!*' said Corless.

Martha said, 'Good heavens! What's that?'

'He's giving three hearty cheers,' said Haig, disgruntled. A burst of clapping came appropriately from the tourists.

Corless turned and looked at the diorama. Under a weird, pale-blue light, the youth and the elders sat round a small camp-fire. Behind them, faintly seen, were the man and the bluish mist.

'Ladies and gentlemen, on to Alchera Seven,' said Rusking.

Still the pervading influence of the Snake, thought Corless, his good humour fading. He could not prevent the feeling that the Snake could explain the mystery. If Rusking had accomplished this eerie effect directly and deliberately, he was a master of the macabre.

Corless shook himself. He was being fanciful. He discovered that Haig and Sergeant Clough were moving off, leaving him alone with Martha. He was on the point of going after them when the girl spoke.

'I've got something to say to you,' she said coldly. 'Leave Mrs Ashwood alone.'

'What the devil!' he said.

'You listen to me, Jock Corless, and no trying to put me off. I work for Mrs Ashwood. Her health may not be as seriously undermined as she imagines. But she was sick when she came here. She became interested in this Dream Time Land, and it's done her good. When she's well and returns to Sydney she'll forget about waking up from dreaming and all she'll be is an expert on blackfellow myths. It's the fashion these days, and it does no harm, after all. But this afternoon you put her back to where she was when we came here.'

Corless recalled the queer change in Mrs Ashwood, but he wasn't responsible for that.

'I did nothing of the sort,' he said.

'Yes, you did.' Martha was determined. 'I saw you give her something. At the lorikeet show. A message of some kind. She read it when we went back to the house for dinner and she's been terrified ever since.'

Corless remembered then. 'That was a letter that came in the afternoon mail. I carried it round till I found her.'

'Ovid Mallet collected the afternoon mail,' flashed Martha.

'Collected it from me after I'd got it from the mail-box,' said Corless. 'Snatched it out of my hand. When the unmannerly swine stalked off, a letter for Mrs Ashwood was lying on the ground. I picked it up. I decided to give it to Mrs Ashwood when I got the chance. I wasn't going to chase Mallet with it.'

'Very well, Jock,' said Martha. 'If that's the way it is, I'm against you. I won't have you hurting Mrs Ashwood.'

Up surged the anger that somehow Martha never failed to evoke in him. He said, 'From a person who keeps photographs of naked blacks in her room, that's good. *Very* good.'

CHAPTER 9

They were alone in Alchera Six now with the night camp under the sacred mountain where the youth and the elders sat round the small fire and the Snake's eyes glowed in the background. The chant floating up from the next Alchera could have been beaten out by those intent figures.

Great is Apma, our father,
Who lives in the Alchera.
Greater than rocks and hills,
Greater than spirits
Who live in the rocks and hills.

'Who said I keep photographs of naked blacks?' cried Martha fiercely.

Already Corless was aware of compunction. And qualms, too. Haig would be ropable when he found out.

'I'm saying no more,' he replied.

'I'll ask Haig,' said Martha, and she went swiftly across the glade, her white dress catching a pale, icy-blue colour from the night light of the diorama.

Corless went after her, but she did not wait for him. Only the occasional glimpses he had of her dress moving ahead assured him that he was not blundering, lost in the Dream Time Jungle.

Then a tremendous shock exploded from his legs to his throat. His muscles locked in mid stride for a split second, but he drove himself on, not looking back to where – he would take his oath – someone stood indistinguishable from the pitchy night. The face, he felt, was the face that had already scared the daylights out of him.

His ear seemed to reach back, but there was no sound behind him. Five more strides and the orange light of Alchera Seven reached in splinters through the bush and he saw Martha's slender form blocked against it.

He hurried on and a second shock crackled through him. This time he could make out a tall figure pressed back into the scrub.

He stopped and said grittily, 'Who's that?'

'Relax, Mr Corless,' said a steady voice. 'It's me.'

A torch flicked on and beamed into a thin, grim face under a slouch hat.

'Bailey!'

'Yes.'

'What's the idea?'

'Inspector Haig seems to think you're not expendable. He's making sure no harm comes to you, though, between you and me, Mr Corless, when he put us here he was hoping someone *would* have a go at you and give us a chance of making a catch.'

'Us?'

Constable Bailey switched his torch off.

'There are four of us along the path.'

'I missed two of you, then.' An echo of something in the earnest young constable's voice caught Corless's ear. 'Bailey, I take it you're inclined to think I *am* expendable.'

'You've got perception, Mr Corless,' said the tough young voice. 'But my views of your value depend on one thing – how you treat Julie Flax.'

'Now look here – '

'Just a moment, Mr Corless. I know what they think of me. I've heard Inspector Haig's comments. I get all the backlash from the fellows, and I know I don't stand much chance with

Julie. But listen, Mr Corless. There's something bad at Ungamillia. I don't know what it is, but if you're for Julie, then I'm for you. And that goes for everybody else – Austin Flax, Rusking, Mallet. Yes, and Inspector Haig, too. I won't keep you any longer, Mr Corless.'

'My humble thanks,' said Corless. 'Maybe you'll excuse me for not kow-towing. I've got corns on the knees.'

'Ladies and gentlemen,' said Rusking, his face agreeably ruddy in the light from Alchera Seven. 'If there is one impression I want you to take away from Dream Time Land, it is that basically the Aborigine has the same feelings desires, hopes, fears and aims as we have. We have seen how, without quite understanding what he is at, he has tried to solve the problem of pain. Now we shall see how he faces up to another great question confronting all human beings, the question of the supernatural – religion, metaphysics, philosophy, if you like.'

'Hoo-ha!' growled Austin Flax, who had popped up beside Corless. 'Give the people fun,' he went on. 'Make 'em laugh, but for Gawd's sake don't preach. Dammit, the Abo's a savage. That's all he is. If y' don't laugh, y' cry.'

'You don't think much of the Abo, eh, old party?' said Haig, popping up just as suddenly.

'He's all right in his place.'

'Out back where he's in nobody's way, eh?' gibed Haig. 'Which reminds me of a question I've got for you, Austin. You bought this place two years ago. Right?'

'That's right.'

'Ever been back to the Territory?'

'Twice,' said the old man. 'Went back for a spell last year an' back again this year.'

'How long did you stay there?'

'Three months. But what do y' want to know for?'

'You can do a lot in three months,' said Haig.

'Gawd! Y' make me sick,' said the old man, and stamped disgustedly away round the back of the audience.

Haig watched him go, then turned irately on Corless. 'You fool, Jock. You've been talking too much. You had to go and sling that photograph at Florence Nightingale. She came at me like a wild cat.'

Corless started to make excuses, but the detective cut him off.

'Okay. It's the way things happen and maybe it won't do any harm. Maybe it'll start 'em talking and sweating and another carbuncle will burst out – Jock, I'll be busy for a few minutes. Keep in the light so I can see you when I want you.'

And he too went away.

In the diorama, the orange light expanded to show Apma, Man and Snake, backs to the audience, looking into a misty darkness in which, somehow, a hint of mystery had been contrived.

'The Aborigine believes,' said Rusking, 'that he has a spirit – a soul. In this case, a double soul.'

A touch on a switch brought two spectral replicas of Apma the Man wavering in the dark mist and behind them two translucent replicas of the Snake.

'There is the double soul,' continued Rusking. 'One part is called the *Arumburinga*, the other the *Ulthana*. Conjoined, they are the *Kuruna*. They are conjoined only when he man dies. The *Arumburinga* is the spirit which stays in the man's *tjurunga* cave. The *Ulthana* dwells in the man until he dies, and then it returns to the *Arumburinga*. After a while, the *Ulthana* selects an unborn chid in which to reincarnate itself and leaves the *Arumburinga* and the cycle of Apma begins once more.

'Now in some way the Aborigine finds it difficult to explain, these spirits can get out of hand. When they do, they cause all the inexplicable tragedies afflicting human life – illness, accident, lunacy, terror, drought, flood, famine. They indulge in mad mischief such as hiding in rocks and leaping out on unsuspecting people passing by and dragging them into the rocks where they are imprisoned for ever.'

Corless detected a movement on the far side of the diorama where the pink dress marked Julie Flax. Someone was talking to her. He watched until a characteristic gesture identified Haig.

Rusking said, 'There are many other actions, some of them unspeakable, for which these undisciplined spirits are responsible, and so the Aborigine takes steps to protect himself from them. He does this through medicine men. It is the aim of every good tribesman to become a medicine man, especially one clearly selected for the position by supernatural power. We are going to see how the youth whose career we have been following becomes one of the special medicine men.'

The demonstration was weird and, to Corless, profoundly disturbing. They saw the youth go to a lonely cave and fall into a deep sleep. They saw the arrival of the spirits of his ancestors, the *Iruntarinia*, who threw a spear at him which passed through his tongue and neck. The *Iruntarinia* then threw a second spear which passed through the youth's head from ear to ear and killed him. After this, the *Iruntarinia* conveyed the body far below the ground, and Corless thought of Mrs Ashwood and her supreme experience.

In the ground, the *Iruntarinia* removed the youth's internal organs and provided him with a new set. He thereupon returned to life and was taken back to his people by the *Iruntarinia*, who were now visible to him but to no one else.

After meditating a year on his experiences, he was allowed to practise as a medicine man. He had the power of death and life; he could afflict and he could heal; he could defend from evil spirits, and he could render one a prey to wandering devils. What Rusking did not point out was that this medicine man's goodwill was as capricious as the lunatic spirits he was supposed to control.

And that, thought Corless, summed up the devilry now menacing Ungamillia. The power of the Snake was supreme. Who knew where it would strike next?

Five minutes later, on the way to Alchera Eight – climbing now as though in the Dream Time Journey they made a circuit on the side of the hill – Corless had the feeling that the Snake had struck and struck where you least expected. He discovered Rusking beside him, breathing heavily.

The artist grabbed Corless's arm and muttered. 'Snake in the rock! Ready to leap out and devour! My God!'

'What is wrong now?'

'I've never known such a day,' Rusking babbled hysterically. 'The police here. A stray black nobody knows appears. Julie on edge. Austin half mad. No, completely mad. And now the Ashwood woman blows her top. "Snake in the rock! *Iruntarinia* screaming for prey!" Of course,' Rusking added as if this explained all, 'Laurie was murdered.'

He trod the winding track, brooding to himself, pushing through the tourists round him. Then he said, 'There'd be hell if these people knew what was going on. Haig and his *atna-arilta-kuma*! What a diabolical trick to put over!'

'Haig isn't putting it over. It came from Laurie.'

'Be your age,' said Rusking. 'It's one of Haig's tricks.'

'By heaven, no! I saw him take the message of Laurie's, arrange the figures of the so-called debts in lines and then substitute letters for them. It took some doing, but he did it, Carl. It was a genuine cipher.'

'No – ' Rusking pushed his face nearer to Corless. 'You say it's genuine?'

'It is genuine.'

'Then,' demanded Rusking excitedly, 'where and how in this place could such a filthy thing exist? Tell me that.'

'Better ask Haig. I don't know.'

'If you *did* know, you wouldn't tell me and it's not fair,' said Rusking. They emerged into the glade of Alchera Eight and he said, 'Well, no matter what happens, Dream Time Journey must go on.'

He strode towards the orange-lit diorama and Haig's voice murmured sardonically, 'An interesting act.'

Corless spun round with astonishment. 'Digger, you lovely beaut! Did you hear all that?'

'Most of it,' said Haig complacently. 'Poor Carl's in a sweat. Get 'em all in a sweat and something might break.'

Yet, when Rusking faced the tourists, he had smoothed his emotional storm out of sight and showed nothing except a pleasant desire to entertain.

'At Alchera One,' he said, 'I told you we could regard ourselves as taking part in an *Engwura* festival, the month long series of ceremonies in which all these myths, chants, legends and secrets are taught to the initiates. We are now going to see what happens when an *Engwura* ends. Alchera Nine, the real climax of Dream Time Journey, tells the story of the end of Apma the great Snake-Ancestor, who had to die as all men do. But now we see the end of the *Engwura* which, in a way, resembles the end of a long and arduous year at school.'

So the diorama, expanding with orange light, showed the declaration by an elder that the *Engwura* was over, the outburst of wild dancing, the frenzied kicking of sacred earth mounds to dust, the hacking and burning of totemic poles, the bursting of the tribe from the long, weary discipline and fasting and prohibitions, the launching into the pleasures of gluttony and women and slothful ease. Chants, yells, screaming laughter, came from the loudspeaker. All the time, Apma, Man and Snake, watched sombrely.

Intent on the scene, Corless became aware that a slouch-hatted policeman had approached Haig. The fact that the policeman was Constable Forrest did not register until Haig turned to him and in a voice rough with rage said, 'Elsie Mannus has disappeared!'

From a hard, fierce walk along the Alchera path, they emerged into a night so clear that if they had thought to look up they would no doubt have descried Apma the Snake in the Milky Way.

The lights still burned in the big house and the cafe was a splash of white light filigreed with coloured lamps. Haig avoided both places. Running now, with Corless and

Constable Forrest panting behind him, he circled the garden to approach the cabins from the far side.

The door of number five was open and the light was on. The interior was a mess. Drawers had been pulled out and the contents dumped on the floor; the wardrobe gaped empty; the bed had been stripped and the mattress and pillows ripped open.

Haig's face tightened until it seemed the fleshy ridges above his mouth were steel ropes. His eyes were bleak and baleful.

'A lovely watch you kept,' he said to the policeman. 'A mob of buffaloes tramp round in here and you don't know it. Damn you to hell!'

Constable Forrest flinched painfully.

'Sir,' he said shakily. 'I was here all the time, and I didn't hear anything out of the way.'

'You wouldn't,' said Haig bitterly. 'But you're mighty good at stuffing yourself with pie and tea.'

Constable Forrest was stung again. 'That was up at the house,' he protested. 'Elsie Mannus brought the pie and tea out to me herself.'

'She did? Did she know what you were doing there?'

'I don't know. She never said.' The constable was regaining control of his voice. 'But I wouldn't be surprised if she did know.'

'Go on from there and tell me what happened.'

Constable Forrest swallowed nervously. 'I ate the pie and drank the tea, and I needed them, too. Then I put the plate and the cup down on a tank-stand – Elsie said she'd get them later on. She didn't want me to go into the kitchen which makes me think she knew why I was there. But she didn't get them. Instead, she came out of the house and headed down here and I followed her.'

'Before or after the lights went out in the house?'

'Before, sir. A good ten minutes before.' Forrest took a long breath. 'I remember the lights going out. I wondered what had happened.'

Haig said, 'How do you know it was Elsie Mannus you followed?'

'Well, of course, it was her,' said Forrest. 'You could pick her by the dress, the uniform. It's a white dress with dark-blue facings. I could see it by the light from the kitchen window as she went by.'

'Did she speak to you?'

Forrest shook his head. 'No. She just made for this cabin, walking fast. I was – '

'Just a moment,' said Haig. 'About the Ungamillia people. Were they still in the house, or had they gone back to Dream Time Land?'

'They'd left, sir. By the front door. They went round the south side of the house. I could hear them talking, but I couldn't see them. I was on the wrong side of the garage. And there was a lot of people making back from the cafe at the same time.'

'So you wouldn't know if the Ungamillia people were all together or only some of them?'

'No, sir.'

Corless was thinking back. Ten minutes before the lights went out, he and Haig were searching Laurie's room, which would possibly explain why they had not heard the Ungamillia people leaving. Julie must have gone down immediately after showing them upstairs and, with the others, set off for Dream Time Land.

'Did you notice the Dream Time lights go out?' Haig asked the constable.

'Yes, sir. About two minutes after I followed Elsie Mannus down here. That was before the house lights went out.'

Haig said, 'Okay, go on. You started to follow the girl down here.'

'She was walking fast. I was about thirty yards behind her when she got here. She went in, shut the door and the lights came on. I sat down on a seat out there, about ten yards away. I could hear her moving around, but I couldn't see what she was doing – the door was shut and the window-blind down.'

'There are two windows here,' said Haig. 'The back window's open now. Was it open then?'

'I didn't think to look, sir.'

'No, you – ' Haig swallowed his wrath. 'Keep going. You heard her moving around.'

'Yes, sir. Drawers being pulled out and other sounds like that, nothing you'd think was out of the way. They lasted maybe three minutes, and then there was silence. The lights went out, and I thought she'd gone to bed. I thought that was all right, too, and I sat out here smoking.' Haig gave a sniff. 'Then about twenty minutes later, maybe half an hour – I didn't look at the time – the girl from the cafe called Kathy Winn came looking for Elsie. She said Elsie ought to be in the cafe helping with the wash-up and she knew she was finished at the house. I told her Elsie was in bed, so she said Elsie must be sick. She insisted on coming into the cabin, and – this is what we found, sir.'

Forrest pointed at the confusion. Corless reflected that Constable Forrest had not shown up too well. He had let Elsie Mannus disappear, and it had taken someone else to find out for him.

Haig had been rolling a cigarette that looked like a caricature of a cigar. He got it going, fuming out clouds of smoke.

'Forrest,' he said, 'go back to when you were standing outside the kitchen window. After you'd surrounded the meat pie, I mean. You had a good view through the window. Did you see Elsie Mannus all the time?'

'Not all the time. There were times when I couldn't see her. No more than a minute, mostly. Say, two minutes at the most.'

'Now think back, Forrest.' Haig's cigarette glowed and fluctuated like a signal lamp. 'Think back. Did you see her just before she came out of the kitchen to set off for this cabin?'

Constable Forrest *had* seen her.

'What was she doing?'

'She moved in front of the window,' said Forrest. 'She had her back to me. She seemed to be folding something – a tablecloth, maybe.'

Haig smoked stolidly for half a minute. Suddenly he swore with concentrated ire and Forrest started back.

'No, not you, Forrest,' Haig snarled. 'Though, dammit, you were played for a fool. But *I'm* the mug. I was given the drum and didn't take it – '

Corless did not immediately understand the reasoning that led Haig to his next course of action. The house could have been searched. Haig ignored it. There were the other cabins. Haig passed them by. Elsie Mannus could merely have walked out of Ungamillia, for the wrecked cabin could have been evidence that it had been ransacked. Haig brushed the suggestion aside. There was in his mood and manner a quality of certainty, as though he finally knew where he was going. But it was a dark knowledge, humiliating as well as frightening.

Julie Flax seemed to understand, however. She had come, at Haig's behest, with the police assembled at the entrance to Dream Time Land.

'You think,' she said to Haig, 'Elsie is somewhere in Dream Time Land – dead?'

'I'll bet she's not walking,' Haig replied. In the light from the *mia-mia* entrance, the lines in his face were leaden.

'Therefore,' continued Julie, 'you also think that we – some of us, the people of Ungamillia – are responsible?'

'When did you see her last?' Haig demanded.

'When I came down from taking you upstairs. That would be just after seven o'clock. She'd finished her work – there wasn't much to do for we only had a scratch meal. She was in the kitchen. Then we started off to return here.'

'Which way did you leave the place?'

'The front way.'

'All of you together?'

'I'll have to think,' said Julie. 'Yes, I think so. Austin and Ovid, yes, and Mrs Ashwood and Martha went out first, and then Carl and I followed. We were just behind them.'

'Elsie Mannus did *not* leave the house of her own accord,'

said Haig curtly. 'But someone got to her cabin and tore the place to pieces looking for something.'

'Why, in the name of heaven?'

'You sure you don't know?' Haig was savage.

Under his bitter glance, Julie's face drained of colour. She said, 'All I can say is I don't know.'

'I hope not, for whoever searched the cabin was looking to see if Elsie Mannus had some kind of record on *atna-arilta-kuma*,' said Haig, and set about ordering the search.

Eight torches pricked through the darkness of Dream Time Journey. The sergeant and two constables, Riley and Thomson, beat through the jungle on the left side of the path; Haig, with Constables Bailey and Church, struggled through the jungle on the right. Corless felt sorry for the policeman. He and Julie had the comparative ease of the path. He was also sorry for the hapless Constable Forrest left lamenting silently at the entrance.

The sound effects came echoing up from Alchera Eight. Or maybe Alchera Nine. There had been time for the tourists to have reached the last Alchera. Corless had some regrets about that, for he had wanted to see the climax of the show.

They came to the still lighted Alchera One and beat through the brush surrounding the diorama. Nothing here, except the queer eyes of Apma the Snake shining up through the pool of water.

Nothing at Alchera Two, except for muttered oaths from the policemen stumbling through wet ferns and tripping over snake-like vines. Their torches sent broken spears of light through the dark. And still nothing at Alchera Three, though Corless took a severe start when a malignant face stared from where the Snake was using his magic to create mountains and rivers. Then he realised it was Haig, wordlessly cursing the search's lack of success.

They came to the long leg between Alchera Four and Five. Haig was now ranging back and forth across the path, trying to do the work of everyone. Corless was aware of another torch that regularly approached the path and shied away again. Constable Bailey watching over Julie, he realised.

Poor Constable Bailey, he thought.

Julie, who had been in front, lingered until he was beside her. She touched his arm. 'Jock, did you and Haig really see a black in Martha's room tonight?'

Corless was surprised. Then he understood. 'That damned Bailey!' he said.

'Hey!' said Bailey's voice indignantly from over on the right. 'I can hear you.'

'Well, get where you can't,' Corless snapped. 'And keep your light on.'

Julie laughed softly. 'Poor Frank.'

Corless said, 'I suppose he told you everything.'

'If you mean the photograph you and Haig found – yes. Was it very dreadful?'

Corless did not reply straightaway. He had begun to wonder about the way Constable Bailey could progress through the undergrowth without a light. He couldn't pick out the noise Bailey made. But branches were crashing and creepers ripping all around now. Haig was getting more action.

'The photograph was horrible,' he said.

Her hand stayed on his arm. She pulled him to a stop. 'Jock, were you really in love with Martha?'

He turned his torch so that he could see her face. Her expression was interested, but mild and unworried.

'After a fashion,' he said.

'She *is* a nice girl, Jock.'

'I guess she is,' said Corless. 'But I don't want to talk about her. I don't want to think about her. You don't want to think about anything that will hurt you.'

'Sometimes you can't help it,' said Julie wistfully. 'Like Laurie and me.'

'Like Laurie and – What's that?'

'Jock' – her voice quivered – 'I've got a dreadful feeling I might have saved Laurie. He wanted to talk with me this morning. He said it was important. But I was in the car ready to go into Winonga – I was waiting for Ovid to come out of the house. I was in a hurry to get away and then – well, you know what Laurie was like. I thought it was just one of his gags. But I believe he could be living now if I'd stayed and listened.'

Her hand tightened on his arm.

'You mustn't blame yourself,' he said, wondering if he was a hypocrite. 'You weren't to know. Maybe it wasn't important at all and had nothing to do with what happened to him.'

'I remember his eyes,' said Julie.

Someone screamed at that moment. It was a wild ululation of terror from away over on the right. Corless's lightning-swift reaction was that the background effects were reaching a new peak. Then he heard leaves threshing violently and a heavy thump, and he knew that this did not come from the Dream Time public address system.

Julie said, 'My God! Someone's gone over the cliff. Come on, Jock.'

She was running as she spoke.

Somewhere in the dark Haig's voice rose. 'Get going, Corless!'

He stared to run. He took two strides, then something gripped his left ankle and he pitched headlong with a crash that shook him from head to foot. He heard his torch go rolling down the path.

CHAPTER 10

Lying on the ground, kicking to free his leg from a vine, he had a momentary impression of something he should have recognised, something that drummed in his mind as if to say, 'Get this straight. See it clearly or you'll be sorry.'

Then the tantalising impression was gone, and he concentrated on getting free of the vine. He dragged himself to his knees, leaning against the slope of the path, and nearly fell over again with vertigo. His head gradually steadied and he crawled round seeking his torch. His hands encountered stones, sticks, damp grass, fumbled among saw-edged creepers, sprang back from the clamminess of a toad, but the hard, cool feel of the torch eluded him.

He stood up and swore. Darkness was absolute except where an orange glow, filtered through a mass of leaves, marked one of the Alchera. The fifth. No, the fourth. Then he realised he could not tell which it was. Where, he thought, are the other torches? He could hear distant voices, but he could not tell their direction and he couldn't see any torch flashes.

He stepped forward and ran straight into a thorn-leafed bush. He angled away and found himself up against scrub. He collided with a tree and swore again. The orange glow was no help to him. It seemed to fluctuate, to be moving. He was exasperated and angry. A man trips and falls on a path – and is lost!

He could yell, of course, but to do so would reveal him as an awful fool, so he kept on moving round blindly. Eventually he found himself on a path, but not the path he had walked with Julie. This was a slash in the jungle so narrow he felt the clinging touch of scrub on both sides.

Remembering that he had a cigarette lighter, he took it out and flicked it on. The dim light showed the jungle wall pressing closely round him and a splinter of a path winding ahead. He debated whether to go on or go back. He couldn't be far from that other wider path. But which was *on* and which was *back*? For the life of him, he couldn't tell. He could no longer see the glow from the Alchera – forth or fifth, which? He decided he would go the way he was facing. He must get somewhere.

He went on, flicking the lighter off for a few seconds to conserve the fuel. He lit it again when he discovered himself trying to push into a thick mass of fern. The path turned back on itself. It repeated the trick in another few feet so that he was more bewildered than ever.

Much as he hated the thought of it, he knew he would have to call for help. He was on the point of shouting when he realised that someone was near at hand. He heard leaves rustle lightly. *Arumburinga, ulthana, iruntarinia?* The eyes of the Snake seemed to glow at him.

After thirty seconds, he moved sideways, the scrub rattling under his pressure. Instantly he was aware of another sound, and he stopped dead. That other noise ceased, but not so quickly. For a second, perhaps two, there was a susurration for which he was not responsible.

He forced himself to speak steadily. 'Who's there?'

There was no reply, but his straining ears caught a sibilant quiver as though someone chuckled not quite silently.

He dropped into a crouch and a hand, a cold hand, lightly touched the side of his neck. He spun round and wrestled with a dogwood branch.

The chuckle was audible this time. He launched himself in the direction of the sound, tripped over a root and sprawled his length in the damp grass. While he lay panting, the cold fingers brushed his face.

'Easy, isn't it?' a voice whispered. 'No one will ever know what happened to Jock Corless.'

He heaved himself up and twisted round. His hands, groping encountered an arm, felt the weave of tough heavy cloth. He seized the arm and pulled, and the next moment was flat on his back, the arm in his hands and nothing more. The thing lay across his chest and his desperate fingers, exploring, found a firmly sewn seam where the arm should have joined a shoulder.

'God!' he muttered.

He instinctively realised that the preliminary torment was over, that the real peril was upon him. He squirmed sideways, his arms crossed before his face. But the attack did not come. Instead, a woman's voice spoke from surprisingly near at hand.

'Who's that? What's going on?'

If her voice was an indication, Martha Rea was scared clean through.

Behind Corless was a soft rustling that receded rapidly and ceased.

Martha spoke again. 'Who's there?'

'My word!' said Corless. 'I'm glad to see you – I mean, hear you. Where are you?'

'Here, on the path. Where are you?'

'Where's the path?'

'Judging by your voice, about four paces from you.'

Which was all it proved to be when Corless pushed through a tangle of creepers and scrub. He stepped out on to the pat and descried the pale glimmer of a light-coloured dress. He moved closer and a whiff of 'Mystique' trailed to him.

'Thank you,' he said.

'Why?'

'You saved my life.'

Reaction set in suddenly. His flesh crawled as he thought of the cold touch on his skin, the false arm probing at him, the evil chuckle and the whispered menace.

'What happened?'

Her tone was still frightened.

'I got lost – '

He gave her a quick account of the terrifying minutes.

'Let's get back to Haig, then,' the girl said.

'Just one moment,' he said. 'How did you come to be here in the nick of time?'

She said reluctantly, 'There was a wild yell. The others, Haig, the policemen, Julie, appeared at Alchera Nine, but you didn't come. I – something made me come and look.'

'I'm glad you did,' he said.

'Let's get back to Haig.'

'How are you going to find him in this darkness?'

'I know my way round here blindfold,' she said. She started off, then she returned to him and her hand lightly brushed his shoulder. 'I'm sorry, Jock. You're lost here. If you can bring yourself to hold my hand, I'll lead the way.'

Her tone flicked him on the raw, but he took her hand and they started along the path. She guided him round the bends as though the sun shone clearly. At Alchera Five, the diorama light showed her face. He felt he could have regretted the old quarrel.

They went past the next two Alcheras, but just beyond Alchera Eight Martha stopped to listen. The wailing of grief-stricken natives droned through the trees.

'Alchera Nine,' she said. 'The death of Apma.'

Corless had an uneasy thought. 'That yell,' he said. 'Didn't it upset things?'

'It did, rather, but Ovid Mallet – he was speaking then – hid his own shock and told the tourists the yell was part of the atmosphere for the Snake.' She pondered for a few seconds. 'There's something I want to ask before we get back with the people. The photograph Haig says he has, why wouldn't he show it to me?'

'When did Haig tell you about that?'

'Alchera Seven. Remember' – she hesitated somewhat – 'I told you I was going to ask him. But why wouldn't he let me see it?'

'Surely you can guess.'

'Obscene?'

'Very much.'

She caught her breath. 'You found it in my dressing-table?'

He nodded.

Her breast rose and fell. That confounded 'Mystique' was very noticeable.

She said, 'I want you to know I know nothing about it. They – someone must have put it there.'

'Someone with a black face.'

'There's no one with a black face at Ungamillia,' she said angrily.

'What about the black in the Fire Dance scene? Haig and I saw the man in your room and it was the same black.'

'And I tell you – ' She stopped and quickly changed direction. 'Haig's a policeman investigating a murder – your cousin's murder. I have no desire to be under suspicion. Would you like to see me involved? Unjustly?'

'No, I'm damned if I would,' said Corless emphatically. 'Heavens, I'd – '

She asked curiously, 'You'd what?'

'It doesn't matter,' he said. That blasted perfume was too close. 'Let's get on and find Haig.'

'He can wait a while yet,' she said, peering into his face. 'There's something else. What is this *atna*-something Haig mentioned?'

'*Atna-arilta-kuma*,' said Corless.

'What does it mean?'

He was sorry because of the darkness, for he wished he could see her face.

'It's a pretty horrible thing,' he said. 'You don't want to talk about it.'

'I'm a nurse, you know.'

'It's the way young lubras are initiated. It's not very nice.'

She was silent for a while, then she said, 'It means nothing to me.'

Corless said, 'Thank heaven for that.'

'Why the fervour?'

He said, 'Let's talk no more about it. The sooner we get to Haig the better.'

The path turned and wriggled up hill and then debouched on to a broad rising drive. When the drive levelled and widened into a large plat illuminated by the orange glow from a diorama on the right, Corless realised where he was.

It was here that he had his first view of the ugly black face. The diorama had been skilfully screened by bushes then. On the left was the waist-high meshed fence that protected the edge of the cliff. He could just make out, beyond the fence, the broken top of the huge dead tree that rose through the leaves far below. Just a few yards from here he had first encountered Austin Flax and talked to Carl Rusking.

In a manner of speaking he could say he was back where he had started.

Intent and quiet, the tourists watched the diorama where, in the yellow light, rows of dark figures sat bowed round the dead Apma who had been placed in a sitting position, his arms resting crosswise on his knees and his chin resting on his arms.

Somehow Rusking had caught all the final emptiness of death in the face of Apma the man. But the Snake was still alive, the eyes molten with the weird powerful mental light that had marked them at every Alchera. From the loudspeaker issued a chant:

> *Wha! Wha! Wha! Wha-a!*
> *Apma, Oknirrabata, that wise old fellow,*
>   *He is dead.*
> *He made the mountains,*
> *He made the waters,*
> *He made the sky.*
>   *He is dead.*

Rusking must have resumed control for it was he who spoke, Mallet standing unobtrusively at the switchboard.

'Even the Great Ancestor with his power and magic, his wisdom and strength, cannot escape the common end of all living things. This, the last myth of the Dream Time Journey, reveals how the native accepts the fact of death. Apma's *Arumburinga* will live for ever in the *tjurunga*, in all the sacred memorials, stones, hills, trees, which mark the course of his wanderings; his *Ulthana* will go out to be reincarnated, return after a time, go out again and again so that Apma will always be alive in the form of man and snake; but the bubble of consciousness and intelligence and thoughts and feelings that was Apma in the Dream Time has been pricked. So, though they chant of his greatness, of his creations, of his deeds, they always return to the refrain, *He is dead.*'

Julie Flax tapped Corless's elbow and whispered, 'Where on earth have you been?'

'I've been lost,' replied Corless.

Julie looked beyond him at Martha.

'And Martha found you?' she said with, queerly, a quiver of amusement in her voice.

'She did, as a matter of fact.' Corless changed the subject. 'What was that yell that started everybody off? You thought – '

'I thought someone had gone over the cliff,' said Julie. 'I was wrong, thank heaven! Nobody seems to know what the yell was. I thought you were right behind me till I got here. If I'd known, I'd have gone back.'

'Somebody did – '

Corless became silent under impatient protests from nearby tourists. The scene in the diorama had changed to the burial of Apma. His wife, his sons and the tribesmen were decorated with the pipeclay of mourning. The earth was poured into the grave and heaped so that one side was short and sharp and the other long and gentle.

'The easy slope,' explained Rusking, 'points towards Apma's *tjurunga* cave so that Apma's *Ulthana* will know which way to go when it leaves his body to rejoin the *Arumburinga*. But that will not be for another year, maybe eighteen months.

The *Ulthana* must first be satisfied that sufficient respect and grief are being expressed for Apma.'

The sound system gave forth with frenzied cries and chants. A shadow moved at the side of the diorama, became Austin Flax looking out over the audience. Someone jolted Corless's arm.

'Where the hell have you been?' said Haig, his face drawn and tired.

'Getting out of a mess.'

Julie came closer to listen.

'What was the mess?' demanded Haig, giving her a dark look.

Corless told him and as he talked tension returned to him, the strain of the icy chuckle and the voice that whispered, '*Easy, isn't it? Nobody will know what happened to Jock Corless.*'

'Jock, you're making this up,' said Julie, and the background sounds covered the horror in her voice.

'I'm telling you what happened,' said Corless. 'I'd have been done if Martha hadn't come along. Whoever it was took to his heels.'

'Florence came along, eh?' said Haig. 'A wonderful coincidence.'

'She came because she noticed I was missing,' said Corless warmly. 'She came looking for me.'

'How do I know it wasn't Florence who whispered in the dark?' said Haig with soft menace.

Only afterwards did Corless realise that Martha displayed no resentment against this inverted accusation. At the moment, he was too angry to notice.

'Look at her dress, Digger. Does she look as though she's been wrestling in the scrub?'

Haig surveyed the girl grimly. 'Okay, for the time being,' he growled. 'Where's this false arm that came pawing you in the dark?'

'I threw it away. Dropped it as though it was a snake.'

'A pity.'

Haig said no more. The dioramic scene had changed again, the recorded chants had been silenced and Rusking resumed with a climactic throb in his voice.

'It is a year since Apma died. In that time his grave has been deserted. Pressed down by his body, the *Ulthana* has waited for the mourning ceremonies to be completed. Now the moment has arrived for it to leave Apma's mouldering remains and depart for the *tjurunga* cave.'

The tourists viewed the tribesmen and lubras dancing round and over the grave, doffing their mourning decorations, tearing them to pieces and stamping the pieces into the mound, saw the mourners strike themselves with digging sticks until the blood flowed, Apma's widow making sure she outdid all others in bleeding. Then they saw the *Ulthana* at the point of emerging from the grave – Corless wondered how Rusking managed this – and setting out for the *tjurunga* cave. They saw the grave deserted, never to be re-visited by the tribe, and then, finally, they saw only Apma the Snake against a background of darkness, the glowing eyes supremely wise, eternally inscrutable.

'Apma is dead,' said Rusking. 'But Apma lives to provide a tremendous unity for his people so that no man of his totem will be tormented by how, when, where, why. In any time, in any place, the men of Apma are at home, and that is – isn't it? – the hope of all humanity. Thank you, ladies and gentlemen.'

The applause was long. When it ceased, Mallet took over to give instructions concerning leaving Dream Time Land. The broad drive would take the visitors back to the *mia-mia*. They would have no difficulty in following it, for there were lights every few yards. He wished them well and hoped that they would return to look at Dream Time Land again.

Haig listened impatiently to these epilogic remarks. When the tourists began to move, he worked swiftly through the throng, every now and then tapping someone on the shoulder. He got them, one after the other; old Austin, Mrs Ashwood, Mallet, Rusking, and each came back to where

Corless waited with Julie and Martha. When the last tourist had departed, they stood in a silent, puzzled group, and behind them like guards were the Winonga police.

'I'll have all lights on,' Haig said to Rusking.

Then through the bright orange glow, stepping carefully to avoid Rusking's models, he led them past Apma's deserted grave to the final effigy of the Snake in the background.

Elsie Mannus lay behind the Snake. Her brown hair curled mistily over her face, but it did not hide the manner of her dying. Her head was turned so that the pulped wound just above the left ear was visible. So was the blood that had streamed over her shoulder and soaked into her white, blue-edged uniform.

Mrs Ashwood went down in a dead faint.

Only Haig and Corless stayed at Alchera Nine. Corless waited in the glade while Haig moved round the funeral scenes looking, among the small Aboriginal figures, like a gold-embossed giant. His head turned from side to side like that of a questing hound.

The place was silent. Corless thought of the people Haig had sent away; four policemen carrying Elsie Mannus on an improvised stretcher; Austin, Rusking and Mallet escorting Mrs Ashwood back to the house; Martha and Julie – accompanied by Constable Bailey – going first to the place where the whispering voice had menaced Corless. Haig wanted the false arm and Martha said she knew exactly where the attack had occurred.

The detective spoke suddenly. 'Come here, Jock.'

He had his torch out, shining it into the fringe of the jungle on the south side of the diorama. When Corless joined him, he was looking at what seemed to be a long piece of piping hidden in the grass.

Giving the torch to Corless, he bent and picked the piping up, a more difficult task than he anticipated because, when he finally had it out in the branch-free space of the diorama, it proved to be more than twenty-five feet long. On one end was a large hook, on the other a strong leather loop.

'Get a feel of it, Jock.'

Corless was astonished by the lightness of the metal rod.

'Duraluminium,' said Haig. 'But what would they use it for?'

'No idea.'

'File it under Minor Mysteries,' Haig said. 'I'll ask Rusking about it later on.'

He replaced the rod where he had found it, retrieved his torch and led the way back to the glade, turning the torch restlessly so that the beam of light flickered over the drive, the canopy of leaves, the fence on the cliff-edge, the tall, dark, ruined-tower tree.

'The poor kid,' he said, and Corless, looking at his softened features, wondered how it was as he had thought of Haig as ugly. Certainly not as he stood there, his cock-a-hoop manner gone, regretting a girl whose life had been stolen.

'Why was she brought here, Digger?'

'The reason could be right in front of us.' Haig turned his back on the diorama. 'A wacky reason. But your cousin's death was wacky – why go to the trouble of staging an accident when a far easier method would have been to make him disappear? There was wacky psychology in that. A morbid pressure away from a place the existence of which must not be suspected. The reason is obvious now we know *what* that place is, even though we don't know *where*. Following me?'

Corless nodded.

'Now there's been a psychological rebound,' Haig continued. 'They've realised the mistake made with Moore. They won't make a second mistake like that. Elsie Mannus *will* disappear. But they're trying too hard again and they make two slips. Or rather, really one, for both are due to *lack of time*. In their haste, they forget I'm not far behind even though I've been caught with Greek gifts.'

A horrible thought came to Corless.

'You mean – '

'Name no name,' interrupted Haig.

Corless glanced round quickly. The jungle seemed to press more thickly round the orange glow of Alchera Nine.

Haig turned and held the torch steady on the fence. The light picked out the strong piping which formed the posts and bearers, the heavy mesh, and, beyond, the great column of the dead tree rising out of the abyss. The detective leaned over the fence and directed the light on the matting of tree-tops forty feet below.

'If there'd been time,' he said, 'Elsie would have gone over there. Hard to find her then. It could be a hundred feet or more to the bottom. Who can tell how high those trees are down there? I thought it had been done when I heard that yell. But there wasn't time and she was hidden behind the Snake. A bad slip, seeing we already knew of *atna-arilta-kuma* and were looking for the place where you go *underground* as Mrs Ashwood said.'

He directed the torch down the cliff again. The light showed rugged shattered planes of slate-like rock pitching vertically until they vanished in the tree-tops.

'To throw the girl down there,' said Corless, 'would leave a track through those leaves.'

'I don't know that *throwing* was intended,' said Haig, and something of his flamboyant bushranging air was back. 'Hold the torch and watch this, Jock. But' – he paused and looked at Corless – 'even with this I can do nothing. I can't prove a thing until, as I told you before, we find the place of the supreme experience. And maybe even then – '

He stopped uncertainly, the trace of cock-a-hoop manner lost.

'But what is it, Digger?'

Haig fiddled a moment with the post immediately on his left, moved to the post on his right, returned to the middle and tugged. One panel of the fence swung back as if on a hinge and lay flat on the ground.

CHAPTER 11

Suggest a good reason,' said Haig, standing over the lowered panel, 'why there should be a gap in a fence supposed to keep people from falling over.'

Into the mind of Corless, the orderly trader, leaped an obvious explanation.

'Junk, Digger. Down it comes in carloads and over it goes. Wish I had something like this in *my* backyard.'

Haig took the torch, lay flat on the ground and peered over the edge. 'No, it's not a rubbish tip,' he said, after a few seconds. 'Some of the rubbish would stick in those trees. And heavy stuff would break through and leave gaps. No, Jock.'

Seeing only the smoothly swelling masses of foliage, Corless was compelled to agree.

'I see one reason only,' said Haig. 'They want to go down there. And why should they want to do that?'

Corless was aware of the death scenes fixed in orange silence, of the burning-eyed Snake, of the jungle background. Only immediately above the dead tree were stars visible.

He shivered and said, 'Digger, if this gap is a way over the cliff, tell me how do they get up and down?'

'Yair, a fair question,' said Haig, hoisting himself erect. With Corless's help, he raised the panel and fixed it back in is clamps. 'I don't know the answer,' he said. I haven't a clue. I'll have to think it over – '

He snapped the torch out, pushed it into Corless's hand and whispered, 'Someone coming, Jock. Hold this till I want it.'

Then he was gone into the bush. Corless stood tautly, conscious of the glow reaching him from the scene of Apma's death. The orange light was like a huge hypnotic eye embedded in blackness. He became aware of something else; the lights marking the drive to the entrance were out. He could have sworn they were burning a few minutes back. He heard stealthy sounds from a short distance up the hill. A few seconds later, there was a crash in the undergrowth and a yell. Then Haig was bellowing.

'The torch, Jock!'

Corless ran towards the commotion with the torchlight trembling ahead of him. He found the detective sitting astride a writhing form. Beaming the torch down, he saw a very familiar face.

Haig slowly released his victim. 'The great lover!' he said.

Constable Bailey sat up coughing and massaging his throat. After a while he clambered to his feet and muttered, 'You might have warned a man, inspector.'

'Warned you!' roared Haig. 'What are you creeping through the bush for? Why not walk on your legs like a man?'

Bailey found his slouch hat, smoothed the brim, patted the crown and jammed it on his head.

'I'll tell you why,' he said sullenly. 'I'm scared, that's why. That black who jumped in and out of the Fire Dance. The false arm that was poked at Mr Corless. Yes, and the dead girl. And another thing. The lights in the drive are out. That's why I was creeping.'

Haig surprised Corless by ignoring the matter of the drive lights.

'So you found the false arm,' he said.

Constable Bailey nodded stiffly. 'Mr Corless's torch, too,' he said.

The detective ruminated a while. 'What are you doing here, anyway?'

'The sergeant sent me. The Ungamillia people are getting restive. They don't like being herded in the lounge like prisoners. And if you ask me,' Bailey added darkly, 'I don't blame them.'

Haig's comment on this would have melted the South Polar ice cap.

Two hours later, Corless went to his room, switched on the light and dropped thankfully on to his bed. He loosened his tie and breathed deeply, trying to make his mind a blank to the memory of the scene in the lounge.

But he could not dismiss the pictures that came in quick hot snippets; Martha Rea's wary caution; Mallet's hate; Rusking's angry bewilderment; Mrs Ashwood's desperation; Julie's soft-eyed misery; Austin's sudden rages; the squawks of Genghiz Khan perched on Austin's shoulder.

Haig's performance had either been superb or brutal – it depended on the point of view. He opened by describing in detail how he had worked out Laurie Moore's ciphered message, and then he rasped the Ungamillia people with its implication. Somewhere in or around Ungamillia, the more esoteric and erotic portions of the Apma cycle were practised upon selected victims who were photographed in grisly circumstances – photographed with infra-red film so that, probably, they did not know they were being photographed and then were blackmailed.

To make his point, Haig produced the photograph found in Martha's room and, first covering a part of the picture with a large thumb, showed it round, indicating the characteristics of infra-red photography.

Martha was white-faced, but she refused to comment. She said she had already told Haig what she had to say on the subject.

Haig then referred to the photograph Corless had seen dropped by Mallet. This caused Mallet to leap up, fulminating dramatically. Corless was a liar. If there was anything in

Haig's allegations, Corless was the man to ask. He was Laurie Moore's cousin.

Cutting Mallet short, Haig veered without preamble into the matter of the gap in the cliff fence. If he had hoped to catch them off balance, to find a weak spot in a flickering eye or caught breath, he was disappointed.

'What gap?' Julie asked, and Haig told them.

It was the first they had heard of it. Austin said that the fence was already in position when he bought Ungamillia just over two years before. Yes, he and Carl had erected the high double-barrier round Dream Time Land, but the fence on the cliff had been built by the previous owner, a man named Downes. He suggested that Haig get in touch with Downes.

Haig said he would get in touch with Downes, and then he broached the death of Elsie Mannus.

This time there was a palpable result.

Sitting on his bed, Corless found his hands damp as he thought of the abrupt stiffening of expression on every face. It was as though an invisible hand had jerked a cord and they had all been turned into marionettes as immobile as the dark figures in Dream Time Land.

Yet – if their evidence was accepted – it was impossible for any of them to have harmed Elsie Mannus. Their stories dovetailed neatly. The accounts of their movements from the time they reached the house from Dream Time Land until the time they claimed the waitress left the house to return to the cafe and from then on to the finding of the girl's body at Alchera Nine so fitted together, that, if true, each was in view to at least two of the others all the time.

On this point Haig was meticulously insistent. He checked the stories in detail; the activities in the house, the return to Dream Time Land, the positions and movements when the Dream Time lights were out – which was when, Haig claimed, the girl was carried into Dream Time Land – the positions and movements at each of the Alchera.

Only one weakly supported statement appeared. Martha could find no one to vouch confidently that she was at the last Alchera before she went back looking for Corless. But, in regard to Elsie Mannus, this did not matter because the waitress had been killed and her cabin ransacked long before.

'Killed,' Haig said, 'with a blow on the head from a club such as one of the waddies hanging in the hall.'

'But killed where?' Julie objected. 'The police have searched the house from top to bottom and there's no sign of blood.'

Haig did not reply at once. Corless realised from his dark, harassed face that his mind was testing timetables and working out moves in a devilishly complicated manoeuvre.

'She died in the house,' he said. 'The person Constable Forrest followed to the cabin was *not* Elsie Mannus. But that's not vital at this moment. The girl's dead. Where's the false arm?'

The false arm was duly produced and examined. Looking at the ridiculous object and recalling his terror in the dark bush, Corless was startled when Austin Flax burst into laughter.

'Seen that before,' said the old man. 'Laurie made it. Used to have fun with the girls sittin' outside in the dark. He had it fastened to a long stick an' the girls used to wonder whereinell the hand come from playin' with their ankles.'

'Quite a wit, Laurie,' said Haig. He looked at Martha. 'The last think you did to him was smack his face, wasn't it, Nightingale?'

Martha's face was fiery.

Haig looked at the arm contemptuously, then threw it aside. 'Moore's dead,' he said. 'He didn't use it tonight.' Before the dreary, nerve-sapping examination ended, Haig touched upon the subject of Rusking's models. He wanted to know where was the workshop in which the models were manufactured.

They trooped out to a room in the outbuilding behind the house. They looked at Rusking's apparatus, at his preliminary sketches, at half-finished figures, at models that had been discarded. The place seemed full of small black tribesmen and background scenes of mountain and plain. There was also one very good model of the Snake, wise-eyed, inscrutable, melancholy.

To Corless, the only significant result from this inspection was the statements made to him as an aside while Haig poked into the exhibits.

First, Rusking, tense, hot-eyed:

'This smashes everything, Jock. Old Austin gets the credit but Dream Time Land is *my* inspiration. And it's ruined because of this massacre. I've worked to build these models. To say nothing of all the wiring and lighting and sound effects. Maybe one could live through murder, but this *atna-arilta-kuma* will kill Dream Time Land. Kill it, I say. And a man hasn't got a chance to defend himself. I might as well cut my throat.'

Second, Austin Flax:

'Look, young feller, what's Haig's dirty game with this blackmail business? Man's mad. Dream Time Land is somethin' I've worked me guts out for. I think it out, I get hold o' Carl an' learn him all I know an' we get Dream Time Land. Do y' reckon I'd cruel it with this filthy old-man-young-girl lark? If there's any blackmail, it's got nothin' to do with me an' Carl. Or Julie. It's somethin' between that Mallet coot an' the Ashwood woman an' the nurse she brought with her. It only started after they come – '

A carafe of water stood on the dressing-table. Corless poured out a glass, drank it, then slowly proceeded to prepare for bed.

Someone knocked on the door.

'Yes?' he said.

Julie came in and quietly closed the door behind her. She wore a dressing-gown over her pyjamas. Her dark hair was a soft cowl for her shoulders; her purple-blue eyes were solemnly appraising. She seemed to have become small and childlike, a reduction explained when he realised that she had discarded high-heeled shoes for heelless slippers.

'Jock, you and I have got to talk,' she said.

While he gazed at her, she reached up, pulled away his loosened tie, folded it neatly and put in on the dressing-table. He remained silent while he conjectured at the reason for her visit. The perfume of her hair disturbed him. He saw that his doubt and hesitation puzzled her. In turn he was puzzled by the gleam of mirth that suddenly glowed in her eyes.

'Jock, I believe you think I'm here for a – What's the word? Assignation. Cast the idea from your mind.'

Corless reddened. 'I'm glad I don't have to defend you from myself,' he said.

She eyed him suspiciously. 'Is that a crack? But it doesn't matter. We're wasting time.' She sat on the bed, smoothed her robe and said, 'Give me a cigarette, please.'

He found his case, got out two cigarettes and lit them. 'What's on your mind, Julie?'

'Murder,' she said. 'Blackmail. And Martha Rea.'

'Martha Rea?'

She glanced up at him with smoke misting her lips. Her eyes were opaque.

'I asked you this before and I'm asking it again. What does Martha mean to you?'

'No more than just someone I know,' said Corless, angrily. 'Yes, she does. I mustn't forget she turned up in the nick of time for me in Dream Time Land.'

'Calm down. What would you mean to her, then?'

He became cautious. 'What's behind this, Julie?'

She drew deeply on her cigarette before replying. 'Jock, don't forget someone threw a poisoned death bone at you. Would you mean enough to Martha for her to want to kill you? No, don't fly off the handle. Wait till you hear what I've got to say. You see, I didn't tell Haig everything I saw where you had the adventure with the false arm.'

Corless said gruffly, 'Keep going.'

'You remember,' she said, her eyes very dark, 'Haig sent Martha and me and young Bailey to look for that arm. Martha took us right to the place. No trouble at all – '

'She knows Ungamillia, doesn't she? You could have done the same.'

Julie admonished him with her cigarette. 'Now wait, Jock, please. We saw the place. We saw the crushed bushes where you scuffled around. And we found the arm. And then I saw something else. Frank Bailey wouldn't have seen them or naturally he would have jumped. Martha could or could not have seen them. I saw them and recognized them and decided to keep quiet till I'd talked to you.'

'What were they?' demanded Corless, crushing out his cigarette.

'Just a moment.' Julie pondered a while. 'You remember Haig suggested to Martha at Alchera Nine *she* could have been the one who played hide-and-seek with you, and you asked Haig to look at her dress. Remember? If she'd been scrabbling round in the scrub her dress would have been torn to ribbons.'

'Okay. What did you see?'

Julie went on tantalisingly, 'I don't think Frank Bailey caught what I was doing. If Martha did – well, that question remains to be answered. They were thrown under a bush near the path – '

'What the devil were they?'

She saw the glint in his eyes and said, 'Overalls. What's more, they were *my* overalls. I've got several sets. They're handy to slip over a dress when you've got mucky work to do and there isn't time to change. It's a jolly good thing for me, Jock, I can prove where I was when you were attacked. I don't like my things being used to put me under suspicion. No. But we'll forget that. You can see now it *could* have been Martha in the dark. She's a very strong girl. And, besides, there's the photograph in her room.'

'No,' said Corless. 'I won't have it.'

'Then she does mean something to you.'

'Not in the way you imply. But Martha's not that kind of girl. I know.'

Julie dropped her cigarette end in the ashtray.

'That,' she said, 'is emotional reaction. It may be a good guide, it may not. But what about the rest of us? How do you *feel* about us? And forget about such things as the fact I was in Winonga – or just leaving the place – when Laurie was killed. Ignore evidence and just go on your feelings.'

She had him there. Leaving out Mallet, whose face he had punched and would like to punch again, he could not sense distrust or distaste for any of them. Rather, he liked them. Julie with her orchid beauty; Rusking intent on his work; old Austin with his yarns and independent manner and hot rages and his feud with Genghiz Khan. If he could rely on his feelings, they were as free from taint as Martha.

'I surrender,' he said.

Julie nodded gravely. 'I must tell you this, Jock. Martha and Mrs Ashwood have been here two months. Only since they came have things seemed to go wrong. The atmosphere's changed. I don't know what it is, but I've noticed it. And, Jock' – she gave him a quick bright glance – 'I'd hate to see you hurt.'

'Thank you,' Corless said. 'But, Julie, it wasn't Martha, and I can prove it.'

'How?'

'When Martha asked, *Who's that*? someone moved away through the bush and it wasn't Martha. And then, he said looking at Julie, 'there's the matter of perfume. A still night, no wind. Suppose you'd been there, I'd have known in a flash. And the same goes for Martha. I know the perfume she uses. I gave her bottles of the stuff. No, it wasn't Martha.'

Julie said, 'You were so startled you wouldn't have noticed any perfume. But what I'm coming to is, what are going to do about those overalls? Do we tell – ' She broke off and went on in a quick whisper, 'Jock, somebody at the door!' Then with a scarcely noticeable break, she resumed her normal tone. 'Do we tell Haig or not?'

She continued to talk naturally, all the time gesturing at the door. With her voice chattering behind him, Corless silently approached the door from the side, though there was no need for that as the key was in the lock.

He got his hand on the knob, pulled sharply, went out with a rush and nearly fell over a kneeling figure. It was Mrs Ashwood, whose parrot-hued dressing-gown gave her the look of a plump carnival queen curtseying.

'Good Lord!' said Corless. 'Did you lose something?'

Back in the room, Julie sat quietly. Mrs Ashwood's upturned face was gaunt and hollow-eyed.

'Lose – lose – ' she stammered. 'No, I haven't lost anything. I – I was doing up my slipper.'

Corless studied the hillocks Mrs Ashwood's heels formed under her dressing-gown behind her.

'Quite a contortionist, eh?'

She stood up slowly, her face white. 'You don't understand,' she said.

'Oh, yes, I do,' said Corless. 'I don't like people listening at my door.'

Mrs Ashwood moved away, going more quickly with each step, her head turned so that she could watch him. She was pale but her eyes – or so it seemed to him – had the baleful splendour of Apma the Snake. And then she was merely a pathetic middle-aged woman.

He would have called her back, but before he could speak she had turned into her own room.

He found Julie beside him, her eyes round with rueful astonishment.

'That's torn things, Jock,' she said softly. 'Martha will know what we've been saying before the clock ticks a hundred. But we can't do anything about it. The morning might make things clear.'

She reached up, pulled his head down, kissed him on the lips and hurried along the passage before he could say anything.

He was dreaming that Julie's arms were round his neck, that Martha's hand was on his face trying to push him away from the other girl. In the dream, the pressure of Martha's hand grew beyond endurance and he awoke sweating to find that a hand *was* on his face, a cold stiff hand dragging dead fingers over his eyes.

'God!' he said.

Someone chuckled in the darkness, then the bed-lamp flashed on and there was Haig beside him, wielding Laurie Moore's false arm.

'Awake at last,' said the inspector.

Corless was speechless. Ugly? Haig's was the most unbeauteous, red, odious visage in the world.

'Damn you!' he said, giving tongue at last. 'If this is a joke, you ought to be kicked to death. Hell – '

'It's duty,' said Haig, grinning. 'We've got work to do.'

Corless's watch showed a quarter to one. He had been asleep for no more than forty-five minutes.

'What sort of duty?' he snarled.

'We're going exploring, sir,' he said. 'Come on, out you get. Into your oldest clobber.'

The aggrieved Corless had no qualms in expressing his feelings, but Haig was relentless and presently he was groping for his clothes.

Haig dropped the false arm on the bed and produced a hip-flask.

'Three ounces of Scotch will lift the gloom,' he declared.

Two minutes later, the whisky had effect, and Corless was prepared to follow the detective with lessening resentment. They went stealthily down the stairs and crept out to the front porch, Haig explaining in a whisper that he had thoughtfully made sure the door was unlocked. He led the way round to the south side of the house, warning Corless against the slightest noise.

'Start Genghiz Khan squawking and the whole world will know,' he whispered.

Keeping to the grass, they footed quickly down the slope. The still clarity of the night made a capsule of space. The stars cast shadows and the roar of a truck, grinding up the highway from Winonga, could have been just over the brow of the hill. The irregular black wall of the jungle mounted over them and they saw the tented roof of the *mia-mia* entrance to Dream Time Land.

Sergeant Clough's voice said, 'Who's that?'

'Haig and friend,' said the detective.

'Friend?' muttered Corless. 'File that with the kiss of Judas.'

The sergeant stepped out of the *mia-mia*, another man behind him. Corless made out the vague outline of a police hat.

'Got the rope?' Haig enquired.

'Bailey's got it,' said the sergeant with a chuckle. 'Putting a knot in every eighteen inches has kept him busy. Kept him from fretting over his girl.'

Constable Bailey handed a heavy coil of rope to Haig. He did not speak, but his indignation could be felt.

Haig said, 'Everything else in hand?'

'Church, Felton and Riley,' said Sergeant Clough, 'are down at the back gate. They take turns in walking along the back fence. There'll always be two of them at the gate. Bailey stays here at this gate. Thomson is down at the east corner and I'll patrol along the west end. Not that there's much chance of anybody getting over the double fence,' the sergeant added. 'But if they do try – '

He went to the outer fence and pretended to climb it. The wire mesh was so taut that every movement evoked a twang.

'Nobody will get in,' he said.

Haig and Corless passed through the *mia-mia* and waited on the inner side until the gate was locked.

'Where's Forrest?' Corless asked.

'Back to station duty,' Haig snapped. 'And he won't hold *that* job much longer, either.'

They walked along the drive for a few yards; then Haig, making use of his torch, headed into the narrow path leading to Alchera One.

'Wrong track,' said Corless, who now understood the purpose of the expedition. 'Alchera Nine is along the drive.'

Haig said, 'First there's the matter of some overalls.'

'Dammit! You were listening!'

'The balcony is useful,' said Haig complacently. 'File me under Opportunities Overlooked, Never. Which is a file *you* don't belong to.'

'What do you mean?'

'A girl like Julie kisses you, and you let her get away.'

'Go to hell!'

Haig grunted. The fan of light from his torch flickered over the jungle walls. They went down the flexuous path and silence closed in on them with a tangible pressure. Corless sensed the eyes of the Great Snake peering up through the pond in Alchera One. Another sixty labyrinthic yards brought them to Alchera Two. Alchera Three was behind them after several more serpentine bends. Then they were at Alchera Four, upon which Haig pushed forward for fifty yards before he stopped and sent the light exploring the right-hand side of the path.

'This is where you tripped,' he said. 'And where you rolled off the main path.'

The torch revealed an opening in the scrub, the entrance to a track so narrow one could not walk along it without brushing the bush on both sides. It diverged from the other so gently that for eight yards the timber separating the two was, near the ground, scarcely more than twelve inches through.

Gazing at the spot where he had crashed suddenly revived Corless's vivid impression that he had missed some vital point. Now, reliving the exasperating moments when he squirmed on the ground, he knew what it was that had escaped him.

'Digger,' he said to Haig. 'I thought I tripped over a vine. But it wasn't a vine. I tripped over somebody's foot.'

'What!' Haig was falsely incredulous. 'You've just realised it! You didn't deserve to get out of it – ' He moved into the narrow track, continuing to talk. 'It's along here you played with the dead hand. Yes, round the second bend. If Julie's right' – he gave an exclamation – 'we don't have to look any more.'

Under a prickly leafed bush, the torchlight came to rest on a set of dark-green overalls, lying crumpled and twisted as though hastily doffed and thrown down. Haig picked them up by the shoulder straps and searched the voluminous pockets. then Corless's heart began to beat hard. The detective pulled out a small rolled-up handkerchief from which came the faint but unmistakeable odour of 'Mystique'.

CHAPTER 12

Haig's torch played round the clearing in front of the Alchera Nine. It glanced over the black effigies of grief, gave momentary life to the eyes of Apma the Snake, touched the dark anarchy of scrub, frosted the sturdy fence on the cliff-edge and picked out the tall ruined tree.

'Let's get started,' the detective said as he dropped the overalls and took the coil of rope from his shoulder.

Corless scarcely heard him. He was still under the shock of recognising Martha's perfume on the handkerchief. He was badly confused over the whole matter. It could have been Martha's foot which tumbled him down in the dark. On the other hand, if she had tripped him, why, having started the job, hadn't she finished it? If it had been her ally who played around with the false arm, why had he retreated when Martha spoke? In fact, why had Martha spoken at all? But the fact remained the handkerchief was redolent of 'Mystique'.

Haig said, 'Snap out of it. We're going over the cliff.'

They lowered the movable panel, and Haig fastened an end of the knotted rope round one of the posts. He took extraordinary care over this procedure with the result, so he claimed, the rope would break before his knots yielded. And the rope, he said, would hold an elephant.

He let the rope drop down the cliff to swish into the leaves forty feet below.

'How long is it?' Corless asked.

'Ninety feet, which should be enough. I don't think the stuff down there is any taller than the scrub up here. We should have rope to spare.'

'Suppose it's caught in the branches or it *isn't* long enough?'

'File me under Acrobats, Great and Grand. I'll manage.'

The detective directed the torch to where the rope passed over the stony edge of the cliff. Nodding as though in reply to some private comment, he retrieved the overalls, folded them into a thick pad and tied them securely round the rope so that they would absorb the rock's abrasive action.

'I think of everything,' he announced.

'Huh! What about light? It isn't going to be easy going down there in the dark.'

'Got you, Jock,' said Haig, and even in the darkness his grin was obvious.

From his coat pocket he brought forth two hunting torches of the kind that are strapped round the head. He gave one to Corless. 'We wear these,' he said. 'They'll show the way.'

He fastened on his own torch as he spoke. He took off his coat, folded it and placed it on the ground, and with the coat he left his flask.

'It might get hurt on the way down,' he said. 'And that is not to be thought of. Right, Jock, I'll be seeing you. I'll give a hail when I hit bottom.'

He swung lithely over the cliff. Leaning out, Corless watched his light descend, its white oval dancing distortedly over the broken face of rock. There came the rustle of leaves and the light was obscured. Then it vanished. After that, there was only the jerking of the rope.

Three minutes later, Corless heard the detective's muffled voice.

'Okay, Jock. Your turn.'

Corless went down slowly and carefully, his feet braced against the rock. He encountered difficulties when he came to the trees, but Haig had pioneered the way through the branches, and with the rope and the detective's voice to guide him, he reached the bottom in good time. Haig had judged the distance well for there was a surplus of five feet of rope lying on the ground.

Corless saw a glade of about sixty feet in diameter. The outer edge apparently topped a precipice similar to the one they had just negotiated, the only difference being it was fringed with thick scrub. But the dominating feature of this lower glade was the huge dead tree. It was easily twenty feet through at the base, though its flaring buttresses made it seem larger. Time and weather had seamed the dull grey surface with irregular cracks that penetrated only the fraction of an inch into its tremendous bulk.

'What else can you see?' asked Haig.

'The place has been cleared.'

'Look again. This clear space with the small trees on the circumference, the branches overhead and the dead tree in the middle like a tower – what's it make you think of now?'

Corless looked again and thought he had it. 'A *tjurunga* cave.'

Haig grunted. 'Yuh! But there's something more. Come over here and I'll show you.'

He guided Corless to an outer corner of the plat and faced him towards the tree.

'Get your torch shining straight ahead with mine, Jock. Good. Now what do you see?'

A big rib jutting out from the butt of the tree had a shape that Corless recognised at once.

'The background in the photographs,' he said.

Haig nodded. He stepped forward about five paces, turned and looked back.

'The blacks stood here, I reckon, Jock.'

Corless could almost see the unclothed Aborigines. He had a chilly skin-crawling feeling as though evil had webbed tangibly over the plat.

Haig continued, 'Two subjects and the photographer. At least three people were down here. Think of that.'

'Think of everything else,' said Corless.

'Yes, the place stinks,' said Haig. 'But I want to know how they get down here and how often, and everything they did here.'

'Who are *they*?'

'I could put my hand on them, but' – Haig was grim – 'that's all I could do because I can't prove a thing. Damn! I wish I'd brought that flask down. Ah, well, Jock, let's get to work.'

They went over the glade inch by inch and learned that it had been worn smooth by many feet. They crept through the scrub on the outer side, their torches revealing a sullen cliff that extended far below the range of the lights; they worked round the walls of the plat and reaffirmed what they already knew – there was no way down from the ground above except the way they had come, swinging on a rope.

'Yet there must be another way,' said Haig fretfully. 'Look at that ground. There's been a multitude here by the look of it. Give me your torch.'

Corless took his torch from his head and Haig did likewise with his. The detective went to the dead tree, moved round the ribbed butt and shone the conjoined beams up the mottled trunk.

'What are you looking for?' asked Corless.

'Marks in the trunk where they could have stuck clamps in for holding ladders. But there's no sign of a hole.'

'How would they get across to the top of the tree from up there? It's twenty feet higher than the ground level at least.'

'That?' said Haig indifferently, 'Any fool could work that out. The point is, how do they come *down*? And then go up again. For, I tell you, Jock, the people who use this place don't climb the cliff. I wish I had that whisky.'

The people who used this place? Julie, old Austin, Mrs Ashwood, Martha, Rusking, Mallet? Corless went over them one by one. Were they all in it or only one or two? It was a deadly secret to keep which Laurie Moore and Elsie Mannus had already died. *Atna-arilta-kuma*, he said to himself, and again the air was evilly cold.

Haig also seemed affected by the atmosphere. Then Corless realised that the detective was reacting to something more tangible. He stood in a queer stiff attitude, the torches, one in each hand, jetting out steady beams as though held in stone.

'Listen!'

Corless heard a soft thump which was succeeded by a slow gliding rustle.

Haig broke from his catalepsis, whirled round and shone the torches at the tree-masked cliff. Corless's hair almost stood on end. The rope was sliding down, knot by knot, and looping unevenly on the ground. There came another thump in the leaves above them. Something dangled there, caught in the branches; something that emitted a hissing stream of sparks.

'Jump!' said Haig.

The torches went out, leaving them in darkness rendered doubly heavy by the yellow sparks above them. Corless felt the detective's hands on his shoulders, heaving him round the trunk, hauling him over knobby buttresses, pressing him deep into a cleft between two ribs.

'I hope the tree will stand,' Haig said.

The tree stood, but Corless felt it buck as though a giant hammer had struck it. The explosion was devastating. It redetonated in echoes that went cracking round the hill. The air hissed with broken branches and driven leaves, loose stones rattled down the cliff, and through the unseen murk came the acrid taint of burnt gelignite.

Haig was pulling Corless out of the shelter before the echoes had stopped rolling.

'There'll be another,' he said as he pulled. 'One on each side to make sure.'

They stumbled round the tree and flung themselves into a hollow. Again came the ear-shattering, body-wrenching roar, the short hard jolt from the dead tree, the storm of leaves and branches. Then the echoes died and there was a deep dust-laden silence.

They stood tensely in case there was a third bomb, but nothing more happened and presently their breathing became relaxed. Haig crawled around until he found one of the head torches, but he did not switch it on. They sat in darkness and waited while shouts that started in the distance grew nearer until they were overhead and torches flashed downwards from the edge of Alchera Nine; torches that could be seen easily because the explosions had ripped great patches of the foliage away.

'Inspector Haig!' someone shouted. 'You all right?'

Haig flicked on his torch. Corless envied his bushranger grin.

'Perfectly all right. Why do you ask?'

'Hell!' said another voice, and there was some confused muttering.

'Okay,' Haig said. 'I know. Some bastard heaved a couple of gelignite bombs down on us. We didn't collect. Who's up there?'

'The lot of us – Bailey, Riley, Thomson, Church, Felton. Clough speaking.'

'Good on you, Cloughie. Have a look at what's left of the rope up there.'

'It's been cut through.'

Haig laughed raspingly. 'The fool! Trying too hard again. If he'd thrown the bombs first, he'd have got us.'

'How the devil are we going to get you up, sir?'

'Ask me something hard, sarge, like who threw the dam' bombs,' said Haig wearily. 'Bailey?'

'Yes, sir.'

'You know the house. Get up there and bring down a line of cord, a fishing line or something long enough to reach down here. You, Riley and Thomson.'

'Yes?'

'Set off round the fence. Right round. See if there's a place where it's been cut or someone could get through. And keep together, the two of you. Sarge, you and Felton and Church stay here. We don't want any more visitors.'

'Right, sir.'

'And Cloughie!'

'Sir?'

'My coat still there?'

'Yair.'

'Look under it. A flask there?'

'Yes, sir.'

'Thank heaven the grenadier's honest,' said Haig feelingly. 'I hate thieves. Sarge, make sure the cap's twisted in tightly. Then drop it through the gap in the trees. Wait on. Felton and Church hold the torches and shine 'em down. Come on, Jock, you shine our torches up. Righto, Cloughie. Drop it straight or I'll have your hide.'

The flask came down glittering and turning in the concentrated light of the torches. Haig fielded it perfectly.

Ten minutes later, a fishing line, weighted with a stone, descended smoothly. A minute after that, it returned pulling up the knotted rope. Presently Sergeant Clough's voice announced that the rope was ready for action. Haig sent Corless up first. Corless made the ascent puffing and groaning. He collapsed on the top to let the unaccustomed ache throb out of his muscles. He was still supine when Haig arrived and likewise threw himself on the ground. After a while, Haig produced the precious flask and shared the remainder of its contents with Corless.

Then he got to his feet and the rays of his torch, back on his head, swept over the circle of policemen to linger on Riley and Thomson, who had returned from their tour of the fence.

'Well?'

'We went right round,' said Riley. 'No sign of a break. No place where anybody could climb over.'

'Then he must have come through one of the gates.'

The sergeant stirred uneasily. 'Impossible. The gates were guarded every moment until we heard the gelignite. I showed you the layout. Nobody got through the gates.'

Haig said thoughtfully. 'Getting out would be a different matter. You'd leave the gates – '

Sergeant Clough anticipated him.

'We left the gates locked. And we have all the keys.'

'So you think,' said Haig sourly. His torch shone into Constable Bailey's eyes. 'You had to unlock the gate to get through to the house, Bailey?'

'Yes, and I locked it when I passed through. And I did the same coming back.'

'Where did you get the fishing line?'

'In the garage.'

'See anybody?'

Bailey shook his head. 'No.'

'Yet,' said Haig, 'there were two bangs loud enough to wake Winonga up, ten miles away.'

'Well, I *did* see one light,' Bailey said. 'I guess it was in old Austin's room.'

'Only one light?'

'The garage is at the back of the house,' said Bailey. 'There could have been more lights at the front.'

Haig seemed about to speak roughly, then he apparently changed his mind, for his next words were mild.

'If you're right about the gates and we have all the keys and there's no other way in or out of Dream Time Land, there should be a vacant bed at the house.'

'Not necessarily,' said Corless. 'What about the stray blackfellow?'

'The stray blackfellow?' Haig pondered, and then he smiled wryly. 'The black Austin called Bucktooth Tommy who died fifteen years ago in Alice Springs. File it under Laws, Universal, Jock, that men, white *or* black, don't spring into being out of nothing. Not even the Great Snake could do that,

I guess. No.' He was silent until he seemed to sense that the sergeant and his men were waiting for some words of wisdom. The bushranger looked flared into his face. 'We need a break,' he said. 'Oh, how we need a break. Even now they can laugh at us if they sit tight. So let's go and see what we can get out of Mrs Ashwood.'

The sergeant was astonished.

'Why *that* woman?'

'Because,' said Haig grimly, 'her dreams have turned into nightmares.'

As they started up the drive, a wild squawking arose in the house. Haig gave a disgusted laugh. That famous watch-dog, Genghiz Khan, was easily an hour too late.

The hall lights were burning. Genghiz Khan perched on the baluster and muttered indignantly. Julie, Carl Rusking and old Austin, attired in dressing-gowns, huddled among the conglomeration of spears and boomerangs, waddies and digging-sticks, death bones and *kurdaitcha* shoes. The dominant quality of their eyes was a terror-inspired curiosity. Corless thought he discerned relief in Julie's face when she saw him, but Rusking's and Austin's tension increased rather than abated.

'What happened?' the old man yelped. 'I know the sound o' jelly when I hear it. Two charges. Big enough to blow the place to pieces. Who got it?'

Haig said shortly. 'No one got it.'

'The Alchera?' said Rusking, and his voice shook.

'Calm yourselves, friends', said Haig. 'Dream Time Land is unharmed. Your investment is safe. Jock and I were the target, but we ducked in time. File it under Miracles, if you like. In the meantime, I want to see Mrs Ashwood.'

'Mrs Ashwood!'

It was Julie who spoke, and her eyes held a weird astonishment.

'Any objection?' demanded Haig.

'No-o. But – '

Julie paused while she looked at Haig with an air of cosmic surprise.

'But what?'

Julie did not speak and Austin said, 'She means *that* stupid, mixed-up trollop!'

Julie said, 'I did not mean quite that. But Mrs Ashwood! Is she responsible for all this horror?'

'She had her part in it. Again, any objection?'

Julie shook her head.

She led the way upstairs with Haig and Austin close behind her.

Rusking and Corless came along together and as they put their feet on the first step, Rusking said, 'Jock, what was the gelignite about?'

Corless hesitated. Haig hung poised a moment above them, looking back with fiercely bleak eyes.

'Tell him,' he said.

Corless told the story in six brief sentences and Rusking's face was grey with fright. By this time, they were in the upstairs corridor heading left to the second door on the right from the landing. Mrs Ashwood's room was in darkness, but a light showed under Martha's door.

Haig thumped on Mrs Ashwood's door. There was no response. Nothing stirred within the room. Haig knocked again. A deathly premonition mounted in Corless.

'Wake up in there!' bellowed the detective.

He tried the door and it opened. He reached into the darkness, discovered the switch and pressed it down. Their eyes blinked for a moment in the blaze of light. Corless's fast apprehensive glance over bed and floor was followed by a sigh of relief which he kept to himself.

Mrs Ashwood was not in the room.

Haig strode over to the windows, pulled them back and examined the balcony. He came back into the room, went to the wardrobe and flung the doors open. There was only the remarkable array of Mrs Ashwood's variegated clothing.

Corless heard an exclamation and turned to see Martha Rea in the doorway. Her eyes were wide and astonished. Haig saw her and shouted, 'You, Nightingale! Where's your boss?'

'If Mrs Ashwood's not here, I don't know where she is,' Martha replied coolly.

'What have you been doing?'

'Trying to sleep,' said Martha. 'In fact, I *was* asleep for a while. Loud explosions woke me up.'

'Did they indeed!' said Haig with dreadful irony. 'Okay. Get in here and see what clothes are missing.'

Martha worked quickly. At the end of her examination, she announced that wherever Mrs Ashwood was she was apparently wearing no more than a nightdress, slippers and dressing-gown.

'Right,' said Haig, spearheading a procession out into the corridor.

Corless's foreboding, in abeyance for the last few minutes, revived into fiercer life. Ovid Mallet joined the party at the landing. His mouth was white and his eyes jerky. He kept his hands in the pockets of his dressing-gown. They were shaking, Corless guessed.

Haig leaned over the baluster and shouted for the policemen. They came running up the stairs with the sergeant gamely in the lead. It was almost humorous, thought Corless, that Constable Bailey looked at no one but Julie. Julie did not look at him at all. Poor Bailey, Corless thought.

Haig said, 'Mrs Ashwood is missing, but she can't be far away. Her clothes consist of nightdress, dressing-gown and slippers. She's either in the house or nearby. Look for her.'

It was Bailey who found her. He came upon her in a place which he tried only as a final resource. She was on the floor in Haig's room. Behind her left ear was the now familiar pulped wound and she would never dream again.

CHAPTER 13

The time was then a quarter past three. Twenty minutes later, Haig lit one of his unwieldy cigarettes and settled himself in a chair to listen to Corless's bitter self-reproaches. The confusion and hysteria had been quelled, Mrs Ashwood's body removed and the members of the household sent to their rooms with orders to stay there.

'I should have known,' Corless said. He was bone-weary and low in spirit and his conscience would not let up. 'She came to tell me something and I thought she wanted to listen in. Digger, I couldn't feel sicker.'

'She wanted to tell me something, too,' said Haig, 'and was killed for it. I'm not blaming you, Jock. You weren't to know she came to your door in self-defence. And you've got this consolation – she wasn't killed in *your* room.'

Corless lapsed into uneasy silence. The voice of Sergeant Clough sounded hollowly from somewhere in the corridor. Pulling on his cigarette, Haig eyed the dark stain in the carpet. From there, his glance travelled slowly towards the bed. He stood up.

'What's wrong now?' Corless said.

'Think back,' said Haig, dropping his cigarette into the ashtray. 'How many people came in here when Bailey blew the bugle?'

Corless ticked names off on his fingers.

'Yourself, me, the sergeant. Riley and Church. Austin, Carl Rusking. And Bailey, of course. That's all.'

'Was any of them suddenly afflicted and had to sit on the bed or lie down or something?'

'Good God, no! What are you thinking about?'

'I'm thinking about Mrs Ashwood and why she came here.' Haig's eyes held a hard bright glitter. 'She wouldn't knock on the door – she didn't want to be seen or heard. She would come straight in without putting on the light. She would think I was here asleep. Then she would discover I wasn't here. She didn't have much time for she was killed right beside the bed. But maybe she *did* have time to leave a message, something that would make me understand that she had been here and why. And so she was the one to pull the bedspread back and leave the pillows crooked.'

Lifting the pillows, Haig took out his pyjamas and shook them and dived on the photograph that fluttered to the floor. Corless peered over his arm. There were three people in the dark scene depicted in the photograph. Two were the scrofulous blacks who had appeared in the photograph found in Martha's room. The third was Mrs Ashwood herself.

'Well, by God!' said Corless. 'She must have been completely mad.'

Haig shook his head. 'Not mad enough for this. She was tricked. Look at her dreamy expression and remember she spoke of a supreme experience. In a place made sacred by demonstrations of the true magic of life. Yair, she was tricked. Decked out like a Kukatju lubra and photographed with no idea of what was happening. She thought she was alone with the influences of the *Iruntarinia*. After a while someone would come to her and put her through some Myall mumbo-jumbo, and the first she would know of what really happened was when she got this.'

Turning the photograph over, Haig read aloud the words scrawled on the back:

You can have the negative of this for £2,000. If you don't want it, copies will go to certain of your prominent friends in Sydney. If you do want it, you will be told when and how to hand the money over.

'This,' said Haig, 'is blackmail *atna-arilta-kuma*.'

'And I gave it to her,' said Corless, recalling the envelope with the stiff enclosure.

'Yair, so she thought you were the blackmailer, or you could have been the blackmailer, which is why she wanted to speak to you tonight. She decided she'd get it over, finished one way or another. But you were engaged, so to speak. In the circumstances, she was justified in a spot of eavesdropping. She went back to her room and thought about it and decided to come to me. Yair, you gave it to her, Jock, but who was so eager to collect the mail?'

So much had happened that the fierce little quarrel with Mallet at the mail-box had receded into the far background of Corless's mind.

'Ovid Mallet,' he said.

'Yair.' Haig's eyes sought Corless speculatively. 'I'll remind you of something else about Mallet. He dropped a photograph in front of you at the cafe.'

'I remember. He called me a liar about it.'

'If you had a blackmailing photograph in your possession, do you think you'd be such a damned fool as to carry it so that it would be dropped accidentally?'

'I don't – What are you driving at, Digger?'

'Put yourself in Mallet's shoes when Jock Corless arrives at the Well of St Giles and acts in a highly suspicious manner,' said Haig. 'Corless prowls round without letting on who he is. Now wouldn't you – don't forget you're Mallet – wouldn't you wonder how much Corless knows about the blackmailing racket? And wouldn't you decide the easiest way to find out is to drop – accidentally – one of the blackmail photographs in front of Corless and watch his reaction? That,' Haig finished, 'is what I mean.'

He went to the door, opened it and discovered Sergeant Clough leaning against the corridor wall.

'Sarge, I want Mallet. Bring him here. If he objects, you know what to do.'

The sergeant nodded and went ambling along the passage. Haig returned to the room without shutting the door. He rolled another cigarette. He did not speak.

In Corless was a sick nervousness he had not thought possible. But his apprehension was not for Mallet. He had no sympathy for Mallet whatsoever. But it did not seem credible that Mallet was alone in the blackmail scheme. Pictures went through Corless's mind. Julie, Martha, Rusking, old Austin – were any or all of them involved with Mallet? This was the fear that evoked the hurt.

Presently Haig said, 'Cloughie's a long time.'

But he did not stir from his chair. In the strong light, his face had a waxy yellowish look. The tough ridges had sagged into deep tired lines.

Corless heard footsteps and said, 'Here he is.'

The sergeant inserted his slouch hat through the doorway. 'Inspector,' he said, and his voice was shaky. 'Mallet's gone, and so has his car.'

Haig began to curse. When his profanity wore itself out, he said, 'Now there's only one chance left. And a poor thing it is.'

Corless shut the door of his room and locked it. He looked at the pistol Haig had given him as a deterrent to possible intruders – 'I don't want you strewn over the floor like Mrs Ashwood,' the detective had said. Corless did not expect intruders. All the others were locked in their rooms with, presumably, members of Sergeant Clough's squad on hand to see that they did not emerge.

He shrugged his shoulders and stowed the weapon in a pocket. He took off his shoes, turned the light out and stretched himself on the bed. All he had to do was wait until Haig returned. He wished he could sleep, but hot wires twitched in his legs and his head buzzed like a frowsy bullroarer.

Haig was not sure where he was going, but Corless guessed that Mallet's capture was his purpose. Mallet had apparently taken no more than the clothes he stood up in – pyjamas and dressing-gown. He had climbed down from the balcony outside his window, sneaked round to the garage, pushed the car out and then let it run downhill to the main gate. In fact Sergeant Clough had said, there would be no need to start the motor until he reached the highway, an item of information, according to Haig, of the utmost value to no one.

Corless's mind twanged to a grisly dance. Martha and Mrs Ashwood, Julie and old Austin, Rusking and Ovid Mallet, Laurie Moore and Elsie Mannus – their pictures were in his mind spotlighted by the eyes of Apma the Snake. Sleep seemed impossible, but he must have slept for, suddenly out of nothing, came a bang on the door and a voice telling him to open up.

He cautiously opened the door, relaxing when he saw it was Haig standing there.

'Any visitors?' the detective asked.

'Not a one.'

'Fine,' said Haig. 'I'll have the gun back. Get your shoes on. We're going out.'

Corless returned the pistol and donned his shoes. As he descended the stairs with Haig, he perceived four faces watching from the museum-like hall. Old Austin, peering like a suspicious dingo; Martha remote and pale; Julie, whose purple-blue eyes seemed to fill her face; Carl Rusking with fists bulging his pockets. No, five faces. Genghiz Khan was perched on Austin's shoulder.

No police after all, thought Corless. Haig must have sent them all after Mallet. Then, when he and Haig reached the foot of the stairs, he found that he was wrong. Constable Bailey stood in the lounge doorway, his slouch hat square on his head, his mouth pulled into a stiff down curve.

'Good,' said Haig, looking them over. His earlier fatigue had vanished. The bushranger gleam lurked in his eyes.

'We're ready for the clean-up. Come on.' He started for the front door, then he stopped and looked at Austin. 'Leave your pet behind, old party.'

'He's all right,' said Austin. 'He – '

'Leave him here,' said Haig sharply. There's no place for cockatoos where we're going.'

Austin grumbled through the kitchen and put Genghiz Khan in the kitchen porch. The cockatoo shrieked as the door was shut on him.

'Damn you, Austin Flax!' he said.

'An' damn you, too,' said Austin, but there was no life in his voice.

As they went down to Dream Time Land, the red-rimmed grey of dawn dusted the garden with drab light. But inside the gate, the darkness was so profound still that they drew closer together. No one spoke until they reached Alchera Nine and Haig switched on the orange lamps. Rusking looked at the obsequies of Apma the Snake and shook his head.

'Place should be covered up,' he said. 'I'll have to do it later on. Must go round and check everything, too. There'll be more tourists today.'

'Rusking,' said Haig, 'if you go to the front gate, you'll see a big sign up – 'Dream Time Land closed until further notice'. There's a similar sign down at the junction with the highway.'

Rusking reddened angrily. 'Who put them up?'

'I did,' said Haig. 'Rather, I had them put up.'

'You can't do that – '

'I can and I have,' said Haig. 'Come over here and I'll show you why.'

He stalked in front of them to the fence on the cliff-edge, unfastened the moveable panel and pulled it away. His manner was suddenly more formal.

'This,' he said, 'is the panel you didn't know existed, though you've been here two years. And yet, if you look at the clamps, you'll see they show no sign of rust as you'd naturally expect if they haven't been used. But no matter. You know nothing about it. We'll look at the next item.'

He went to some long grass growing near the fence. He bent over. When he straightened up, he carried the long silvery rod which Corless had seen earlier lying near the diorama.

'Now this,' said Haig as though delivering a lecture, 'is an interesting thing. It's thirty feet long, but it's easy to hold because it's made of duraluminium. On one end you see a hook. On the other, a leather lop. The loop is intended to slip over your wrist thus.'

As he spoke, Haig pushed his right hand through the loop, then gave it a twist so that the leather was bound tightly round his wrist.

'If the rod should slip from your hand,' he continued, 'the loop saves it from falling down the cliff.'

But he made no slip when, holding the duraluminium pole like a fishing-rod, he pushed it out towards the dead tree and manoeuvred the hook over the serrated top. With his left hand he gripped a fence post while he wriggled the rod so that the hook, out of sight beyond the broken trunk, turned port and starboard.

'Got it!' he said, and they heard a faint click. 'Now watch this.'

A slab of the trunk, two feet wide and more than twenty feet long, slanted out from the tree as though hinged near its lower limit. Old Austin, staring, muttered an oath. On Martha's face was white incredulity. Julie's hands, clinging to the fence, tightened convulsively and her face was old. Rusking stood in petrified silence. Only Constable Bailey seemed unmoved. He preserved the proper police imperturbability that refuses to be shaken in any circumstances.

Haig pulled until the top of the slab had moved out a foot or so.

'Notice,' he said, 'how easy it is to control. It's beautifully counter-weighted. And notice the irregular edges. You wouldn't detect them among the normal cracks in the trunk.'

To prove his point he pushed the slab back. Even now that the existence of the slab was known, its outline could not be followed among the innumerable small crevices marking the outside of the trunk.

Haig pulled again. This time he did not stop until the end of the slab landed with a foot to spare in the gap left by the movable panel. Now there was a bridge from cliff to tree, a bridge rendered safe to dizzy heads by steel struts across the slab every few inches and steel stanchions supporting a railing so that on each side there was a barrier about thirty inches high.

'Nice work, isn't it?' said Haig.

Austin's mouth opened and shut, but he made no sound. The others did not move.

Haig stepped on to the bridge and looked back. 'This is quite safe. I've already tried it.'

Corless knew then how the detective had spent at least part of the recent hour or so.

Haig went on, 'Remember that poor silly woman, Mrs Ashwood. She was a changed one, she believed, an *illapurinja*. She had been into the ground. The *Iruntarinia*, the spirit people who live in the ground, had taken her there and she had seen and heard and experienced strange magic. Now we're going where she went, and we'll see and hear what she saw and heard. And what she didn't see and hear.'

Martha shivered and said shakily, 'I don't want to go. I – I'm frightened.'

Haig spoke officially. 'The dimmest possible view will be taken of any refusal to come.' He paused to look his pallid listeners over. 'I don't suppose there is anyone who *really* doesn't want to come.'

This aroused no comment. Corless thought that the cold hard morning after a sleepless night had sapped their vitality, leaving them with only shreds of will to resist.

Haig walked across the bridge with Austin on his heels. Julie moved on to the bridge, her purple eyes unreadable.

Martha followed, taking care not to look down. Corless was next. Behind him was Constable Bailey.

Haig halted at the opening into the tree trunk, looked back and said, 'I'm sorry, Bailey. This doesn't include you. Somebody's got to guard the retreat and you're for it. Next time, Bailey.'

The young policeman nodded. He stepped back on to the ledge, leaned on the fence. Under the level hat, his face was thin-lipped and pale. His eyes were on Julie, who did not look at him. Once more, Corless was aware of sympathy for the policeman.

Then he dismissed Bailey from his mind. They were going down a steep, narrow, fantastic stairway spiralling inside the dead tree, dimly lit by small electric lamps strung every fifteen feet. Their feet clipped and shuffled on the steel steps. The smell of dead wood was in their nostrils, and a feeling of revolving slowly in an endless shaft grew as they turned and kept on turning.

Austin's voice was hollow and muffled. 'Digger, I – dammit! How in hell did this get here?'

'But you were looking for it,' Haig replied, his voice echoing up the trunk. 'You and your holes for gold!'

A few more steps and Julie's voice rose. 'Mr Haig, how long is this going on? I can't stand much more.'

'Patience,' said Haig. 'We're almost there.'

Two spirals later, the trunk widened abruptly, the stairway made one full-circled swoop and then sloped almost vertically down to a hard-packed clay floor.

The place was lit by one weak globe. Corless's heart thudded as he took the last few steps, for two men lurked under the stairs. On reaching the floor, he turned quickly and was aware of another shock. Except for their black faces they were concealed under bags draped over them.

'Dummies,' said Haig behind him. 'Forget them.'

Corless turned to survey the tree-cavern. With its sloping sides and heavy buttresses and dark spaces, it had the effect of a chapel desecrated by blasphemy. He saw more black visages, masks hanging from nails driven into the wood. And then the beginning of understanding came, for the masks were identical and each was the face that had peered at him from the bushes on the plat above, the face of the intruder into the Fire Dance Alchera, the face of the man in Martha's room.

'My God!' said Rusking, staring. 'Who'd have thought it?'

His mouth hanging open, old Austin said nothing. Julie and Martha watched Haig, who now displayed no sign of his usual cock-a-hoop manner.

'This is where Mrs Ashwood came,' the detective said. 'But we have an advantage over her. We are not blindfolded. Up there in the dark of the night someone meets her, someone who speaks of the glorious ecstasy which is to be hers, which could come only through secrecy. So she is blindfolded and led here. She must not be permitted to see this place. A door is opened and she is taken outside – '

The detective went to the sloping wall opposite the stairs. Here between two of the buttresses was a wider space than common. He tugged and a door swung in silently.

'Notice,' he said, 'the irregular edges again. The door is lost to outside inspection in the cracks and crevices of the dead wood. Out through here – '

'Digger,' said Austin Flax as though waking from a trance. 'Them faces. They're fakes. Got to be – '

Haig was suddenly quite venomous. 'Will you keep quiet?' he thundered. 'You're interrupting me.'

Austin's hand went up as if seeking to pat Genghiz Khan. Failing to discover the familiar presence, he looked at the hand in bewilderment. But Corless sensed the reason for Haig's display of ire. He had formed a plan of operations and was not to be diverted from it.

'Out here,' he resumed, 'Mrs Ashwood is led.'

They passed through the opening into the glad. Feeble light struggled down through the wide gaps left in the foliage by the gelignite. The bridge was a black bar against the high, pink-tinged clouds. Corless angled round, trying unsuccessfully to see Constable Bailey. He told himself that Bailey would be stretched out philosophically on some soft grass, making up for lost sleep. Then he recalled Bailey's eyes looking at Julie. No, Bailey wouldn't be asleep.

'Out here,' said Haig, 'it is very dark and still, for a moonless night would be chosen so that no vestige of light could sink here, and a still night so that there would be no rustling of leaves. It's underground, you see. The bandage is removed, and then it is suggested gently that Mrs Ashwood disrobe. Maybe that idea has already been implanted in her. There is no place for trumpery inhibitions. In this place of primitive power and mystic experience, the trappings of civilisation must be cast aside.

'Unclothed she sits on a stool and the magic starts. She hears strange chants. They are pitched very softly and she has to strain her ears. Something cold touches her, raising gooseflesh. A mystic red light glows faintly. She discovers mysterious forms motionless beside her. She cannot see them in any detail, which is just as well for her peace of mind.'

Haig pointed back into the tree, at the two dim figures under the stairs.

'There they are. I covered them when I came down earlier so that your sensibilities would not be offended. One of those figures is beside Mrs Ashwood, the other somewhat to the rear. She is aware of their mysterious presence. There is silence, then slowly before her appear in vague outline representations of the more erotic and secret native rites. Almost invisible hands apply native decorations to her body. She is not revolted. She is now one with the primitive instincts enfolding primeval truth. Silence again. Cool hands touch her. A voice whispers that the ceremony is over. She puts on her clothes and is blindfolded again. As she is led back into the tree to make her ascent to the unmagical ground above, the chanting starts again.

> *Into the ground goes the poor one. Wei!*
> *Into the ground with the Iruntarinia. Wei!*
> *Out of the ground comes the changed one!*
> *Illapurinja! Wei!*

Haig was silent for a few moments, the flanges of flesh above his mouth rigid. '*Wei!*' he said as though he spat. 'Over in those bushes there is someone with a camera loaded with infra-red film. It is used while the mystic red light glows and the subject knows nothing about it. But a few days later, a week perhaps, there comes to the changed one a photograph by mail – '

CHAPTER 14

They were back inside the tree with the door closed. The silence was broken by Julie, leaning against the wall.

'I feel ill,' she said. 'I'd like to sit down.'

She looked ill. Haig got two stools from a recess. Julie sank gratefully on to one and dabbed her face with a handkerchief. Haig offered the other stool to Martha, but Martha refused curtly. Perhaps, Corless reflected, she was thinking of the use the stools had been put to. Or perhaps she knew all about it. That was a horrible thought.

His face shiny with sweat, Rusking came to fuss over Julie, but she pushed him away. She would be all right in a few moments. Martha watched this with contempt. Old Austin slumped against the wall, dejection crumpling every line of his figure.

Rusking said, 'Haig, tell us for God's sake what's been happening.'

Still eyeing Julie, Haig said, 'It grew out of Dream Time Land – '

'That be damned! I knew nothing – '

Haig cut the artist short. 'Wait, Rusking. It grew, as I said, out of Dream Time Land. Someone looked at the Alchera and thought of the things that had been left out. It started, maybe, as a kind of new exciting experiment. Let's get a kick out of things. Let's be daring. Let's have some real esoteric fun for a chosen few. We'll get as close to the original as possible. We'll go into the ground. We'll play with sweet erotic fire. Then we'll return to the non-magic ground above with that tremendous thrilling superiority over the poor herd who don't know what we do. File us under Gods, Knowing Good and Evil. Hence this place.'

Haig waved his hand at the rugged hollow of the tree, at the slender ladder spiralling upwards.

'Fine engineering,' he said. 'But simple enough and beautifully secret.'

'Digger,' said Austin. 'I'm askin' who's responsible.'

'Mallet?' suggested Julie, now recovering somewhat.

'We're taking care of Mallet,' said Haig grittily. 'He won't get far.'

He paused, his dark face thinned into a hard mask. He's stalling, Corless thought with a start; he might know who's responsible, but he's got no proof; he's waiting for something to turn up.

Then it seemed as if Haig was not only waiting but listening. One ear was cocked up. But there was nothing, thought Corless, he could listen to.

'I'll tell you who's responsible when I'm ready,' Haig said. 'In the meantime, let's carry on with the development of the underground magic. Somewhere along the line the great temptation comes. Maybe it develops because we sit on a great hill. Like Apma the Snake, we feel as wide and wise and grand as the view itself. We cannot resist the elation of height. So we bring new people in, people like Mrs Ashwood, excitable, looking for sensation. We can pick them out, the right types for initiation into the greater mysteries. We know the ones to select. Not the ordinary kind of bloke, who drinks his beer every night after work and goes to football or the races on Saturday and mows the lawn on Sunday. Not him, but the superior bloke. The cultured type. Extreme austerity often holds hands over the fence with extreme excess.'

Haig pondered a moment.

'So we pick our initiates, take 'em underground, and then – and then it dawns on us how easy it is to make them pay for their fun. We don't make it too hard. We're not going to bleed them to death. And we're not going to make it a wholesale business – just a few good customers to provide us with nice lumps of cash the tax commissioner won't know anything about. Maybe half a dozen victims a year to give us a clear two thousand pounds each.

'And then,' Haig paused again with his left ear turned up, 'along comes Laurie Moore. Laurie is a wild man. He gets drunk, and he loves to fight policemen, and he makes false arms to tease girls, and when he starts nosing around and gets on the track of magic, we think let's have him in with us. Better that than having him blow the place sky-high. It's only a matter of getting an extra victim or two to provide his share of the profits. So we take Laurie in with us and there we make our terrible mistake.

'For, wild and all though he is, Laurie's just an ordinary bloke. Erotic magic is more than *his* stomach can take. He gets into a hell of a state over it, but he knows that eventually he's going to tell the police or somebody – this game makes him feel worse than dirty. So he starts hinting to his friend Jacks, in Winonga, about the state of affairs in Ungamillia. Then he thinks he'll write to his cousin about it. Jock, he thinks, is a steady-going fellow. Jock will help him out. And in case something happens to him, he works out an elementary cipher giving the big clue. Blackmail *atna-arilta-kuma*. And at the same time, he tells a friend of his at the cafe, a girl he can rely on, so that he has two strings to his bow.'

Haig shifted his weight from one leg to the other. His face had a gloss of sweat.

'By this time, we've heard what Laurie has been saying in Winonga and we're watching him. We spot him going down to the Well of St Giles for several more days at the same time and we know he is waiting to meet someone. So we kill him. And there we make our second big mistake.

'We should have socked him and dropped him over one of the cliffs around here – this one, for instance, where this tree stands. The chances are nobody would have found him – at least, not for a long time, and if he were found who could prove he had not *fallen* over the cliff? But we've got this place on our mind. Attention must be directed as far from Alchera Nine as possible, so we stage our *accident* at the Well. Now – '

Haig's pause was a piece of perfect timing. Tension coiled and throbbed and mounted unbearably.

'Now the weakness of our planning shows. We don't allow – we can't allow for the way things happen. We'll consider these fortuitous events serially though not in sequence of time.

'One: Jock Corless shows up at the Well and chooses *not to reveal himself*, though we know who he is. Good God, we therefore think, he's in the ghastly secret too, and we decide he must go with his cousin. Hence our pretty tricks with the feathered death bone and the false arm attack in the bush. Yes, and the gelignite bombs, although the last is double-barrelled attempt to get Digger Haig as well as Jock Corless. You see, we're trying too hard.

'Two: We have unfortunately posted the blackmailing photograph to Mrs Ashwood, addressed – like the others – with a kid's printing set because handwriting and typewriting can be identified. For a week or so, Mrs Ashwood has been living in ecstasy, but we know that as soon as she gets that picture her ecstasy will change to brutal disillusionment. With all the damned police around Ungamillia, we dare not let that happen, so we try to get the photograph back before it reaches her – '

'Mallet,' said Corless involuntarily and found himself the target of bleak stony glances.

'Mallet, yes,' said Haig, not pleased. 'He goes to collect the mail as soon as the Winonga mailman delivers it. But in the way things happen Corless is on the spot and he gets the letters. But Mallet is determined to have them. He snatched the letters after an argument, but goes off without the letter he wanted. Consequently Mrs Ashwood has to die. We get her just in time in my room where she has gone to tell me about blackmail.

'Three: We watch Corless. My word, we do. And it pays off for just after we've chucked the death bone at him, we catch the little waitress, Elsie Mannus, telling him she can explain his cousin's debts. So Elsie Mannus has to go, and here we excel ourselves. With perhaps no more than two of us involved, we kill Elsie in the house where there are at least eight people, two policemen outside and a hundred tourists not far away. While one of us, wearing one of those masks, distracts Corless and me in the house, another leads Constable Forrest on a wild-goose chase and then puts out the Dream Time lights so that Elsie Mannus can be carried to Alchera Nine. If there'd been time, we would have had the bridge down and Elsie would have vanished. But there isn't time. There's only time enough to hide her behind the great Snake. Our planning has fallen down again because of the way things happen.

'Four: We can't allow – and this is the worst of the lot because we give ourselves away unconsciously – we can't allow for the fact that the Winonga police and Digger Haig – I repeat Digger Haig – will be at the Well in a few minutes after we have thrown Laurie Moore in front of Wilson's car. Of course, we react quickly and start improvising. We use those masks to build up the idea some mysterious black is on the loose on the place on a murdering spree. But it doesn't help us at all. If only we'd known the police were on their way to Ungamillia we'd have got Laurie some other way. But we had no hope of knowing. Only Digger Haig knew the police were coming out. No one else knew until ten minutes before the police party left Winonga. Not even the policeman we have sewn up as one of our wonderful mystic circle.'

'The what sewn up?' said Julie shrilly.

'The policeman,' Haig repeated. He turned his head, jutting his jaw at Austin Flax. 'Old party,' he said harshly. 'You told me a whacking big lie.'

The old man slowly pulled himself straight. 'I dunno what you're talkin' about,' he said.

'Oh, yes, you do. You told me – '

Haig stopped and twisted his head up again. This time there *was* something to hear, a sibilation that gradually grew into hard, heavy breathing.

Stockinged feet showed on the steps where the steel stairway finished its last spiral around the tree. Khaki trousers came into view, a hand gripping a revolver, a broad khaki-clad chest, and then the thin face and hot eyes of Constable Bailey.

He came down to the clay-bed floor and raised a hand to point at the stairs. The other, holding the revolver, was as steady as a rock, though his body shook like a boiler trying to hold down an impossible head of steam.

'Get up there, Julie,' he said, and his voice was a croak. 'Get up there at once.'

She did not move from the stool. Her face was suddenly a conflict of bitter planes and venomous angles.

'You fool!' she said. 'You awful fool! He was bluffing! There was nothing he could prove. And now – God damn you for a fool!'

Corless's heart was going bump-bump, bump-bump. He flashed a glance at Haig and caught a blaze of triumph in the dark eyes.

'He wasn't bluffing.' Bailey's voice rose hysterically. 'You heard him say Austin told him a lie. He knows you aren't Austin's daughter or anything like it.'

'You fool!' Julie repeated softly.

Bailey sagged for a moment, then he tightened up again. The revolver moved round steadily.

'Fool or not,' he said roughly, 'doesn't matter now. Get going before I start shooting.'

Haig said very casually, 'Why take her only? What about her husband?'

'Husband?' Bailey cried. 'Who?'

Haig nodded towards Rusking. 'He is.'

The blood went from Rusking's face. He stammered inarticulately.

Bailey's eyes were red. 'Her husband? But it doesn't matter. He stays with the rest. You're going with me, Julie. Get moving.'

'You can't do it,' she said. 'You've ruined it. We can't get away.'

She was on her feet now, but she stayed by the stool.

'You heard what he said,' replied Bailey, his revolver edging in Haig's direction. 'You should have thrown Moore over this cliff. Nobody would have known. That's what I'll do with them. They'll go down five hundred feet. Nobody can get in there. Then we'll smash these ladders and put that bridge back. How will anybody know? Clough and the rest are off chasing Mallet. We'll be just two of those who've disappeared, Julie.'

There was a hell of indecision in her face.

'Julie!' said Rusking. He took a step forward, then stopped as the revolver seemed to dart at him.

'Just a moment,' said Haig, his voice still casual. 'You – '

'Shut up!' Bailey shouted. 'Julie, are you coming or are you staying?'

She took an uncertain step forward. Corless looked at Martha, pressed against the wall. She was watching him. Then he turned back and measured the distance between him and Bailey. Fourteen feet. A fast low football tackle would take him there. He'd probably collect everything, but he'd give Haig a chance to get in. Julie was passing carefully round the other side of the tree where no one could seize her. Bailey's eyes flickered to watch her and Corless thought, Here I go.

Then Haig hissed sharply. The concealing bags slipped from one of the dummy figures behind the stairs. The dummy stepped out, a big thickset khaki-clad man. Julie screamed, but she was too late. An uplifted *nulla-nulla* thudded down on Bailey's head, and then Haig went into action.

When the turmoil ceased, the big man removed the black mask to reveal the perspiring face of Sergeant Clough.

'You took your blasted time,' Haig grumbled. 'They very nearly got away with it.'

'Those bags you hung over me,' said the sergeant apologetically. 'They kept slipping down, so I fastened 'em with a safety pin. In the flurry I couldn't get the pin open.'

Haig's disgust would have burnt holes in the ground.

'Okay,' he said. 'File it under The Way Things Happen.'

Corless slept like a burnt-out log for eight hours straight in a Winonga hotel. He awoke in the late afternoon feeling dry and wrinkled and disintegrated. The way a snake's discarded skin would feel, he thought.

He improved after he had shaved and showered, made more progress when he had a meal. Then Haig came in and helped him carry his bags out to the Goddess.

'You still intent on going home?' Haig said. He was hollow-eyed and grey in the face. He had not yet slept.

Corless nodded. The sooner he was on his way the better; he couldn't take much more of this place. He thought of Martha Rea. He had not seen her since the Winonga police, who hadn't gone chasing Mallet after all, had taken Julie and Rusking and Constable Bailey away. He wondered why Martha had moved out of Ungamillia before he could speak to her.

Haig said, 'I won't try to hold you, Jock, though you'll have to come to Brisbane for the trial. I've made arrangements for your cousin to be taken back to Lake View.'

'Thanks,' said Corless. 'His mother would have liked that.'

They stood beside the Goddess without talking. The town was somnolent in the glow of sunset. A few people drifted leisurely along the street. To the east, Creeping Hill was an abrupt, auburn-tinged mass. Corless thought he could see the green-roofed shape of Ungamillia showing above the trees on the peak.

Also looking at the peak, Haig said, 'We've caught Mallet, you know. The Nambour police grabbed him, heading north. A car being driven by a bloke in pyjamas is odd, even in Queensland.'

'What will happen to him?'

'Strips torn off him. And devilish publicity. But that will be all. He was acting under duress. They had him in the blackmail trap. He knew Julie had something to do with killing Moore – he'd gone into Winonga with her in the morning and he had to pick her up on Creeping Hill on the way back. But he wasn't an informed accessory. Your sudden arrival made him think you were in it, too, which is why he altered the signpost and why he dropped the photograph in front of you. He was writhing in a trap, and he'll continue to writhe.'

'And Austin?'

'Austin was the mug.' Haig wriggled, stretching the weary cramp out of his body. 'So many of these tough bushmen are when they get up against the real city slicker. Oddly enough, though, it seems Julie's and Rusking's trip to the Centre was genuine. That is, Rusking's an artist and they went up there to paint. Then they met Austin on his Monnadea station – separately, of course, for he had no idea they were married. Julie saw the chance. An old bushman with no ties and plenty of money. Play him along and the money would be hers. He had no funny ideas concerning her. As far as he was concerned, she was his daughter. It pleased him to have a pretty woman treating him paternally. Remember how he had her with him, leading the procession to the flame trees when the lorikeets flew in.

'Julie's idea was to get Austin away from the Territory. So came the birth of Dream Time Land. Rusking's idea and a good one. Until, of course, Julie conceived the idea of *atna-arilta-kuma*.'

A hard flame came into the detective's tired eyes. 'Rusking will get ten years for his share in that,' he said. 'But Julie ought to hang. She killed Moore, the Mannus girl and Mrs Ashwood. She threw the death bone at you and she dropped the gelignite on us. And she beat us into the Alchera and planted the overalls with Nightingale's hankie in the pocket. Yair, she ought to hang, and Bailey, too. He swore Julie was in Winonga for an hour yesterday morning. Actually she drove back to Creeping Hill in an old utility – we found it hidden in the scrub – and killed Laurie, after which Mallet picked her up about a quarter of a mile down the road. It was Bailey who gave that yell, then came after you with the false arm; Bailey who carried Elsie Mannus down into Dream Time Land after Julie had killed her in the pantry – close timing that, Jock – and Bailey who let Julie through the *mia-mia* when she came after us with the bombs and then let her out again. It took me too long to rumble Bailey. But they won't hang. We coddle dirty murderers now.'

'And the stray *blacks*?'

Haig slowly rolled one of his monstrous cigarettes. 'There's confusion about that, but apparently they took turns to wear the masks. It was Rusking you saw when you first came, Julie in the Fire Dance scene, Bailey in Martha's room – after he had delivered Elsie Mannus to Alchera Nine. Again close timing.'

A taxi rolled past them and pulled in along the kerb. The passenger, a woman, leaned forwards to speak to the driver. Haig slouched against the Goddess, his cigarette burning like a volcano.

'Julie beat me all along the line until I woke up to Bailey,' he said. 'She beat me to Laurie Moore, beat me to Elsie Mannus, beat me to Mrs Ashwood. Then Mallet cleared out. No wonder! He could read the map. If you knew something you died. But Julie was right, for he left me without a trump. There was no proof, no real evidence that could be put before a jury. By then, however, it dawned on me that Bailey was not merely an earnest young policeman who'd fallen for Julie. But the real break came when I rumbled the duraluminium rod and managed to get down into the tree. It was a matter of bluffing again. Get Clough and the police out of the way, then take the party below, leaving Bailey on top. If he was innocent, he'd stay there; if he was guilty, he'd come down. He came down. Sergeant Clough did the rest.'

'So Austin was really digging for some trace of the underground,' said Corless.

Haig nodded. 'He was away when Rusking did the engineering work inside the tree. Re-visiting the Territory. When he came back, he soon got an inkling of what was going on, and he began to dig. He had the idea of a secret cellar under the house. He never thought of the dead tree. Anyway he's in the clear. He's been hit badly, but he'll get over it. He's still got Ungamillia and he's got the lorikeets and he's got Genghiz Khan. After a while, maybe, he'll start Dream Time Land again.'

'It would be better if he went back to the Territory, Digger.'

'It's his own business whatever he does.' Haig dropped his cigarette into the gutter. He brought himself erect, forcing the weariness out of his face. 'So you're going home,' he said.

'Yes.'

Haig ran his hand along the Goddess's sleek hood.

'Plenty of room in these buses, Jock. And you've got a long run ahead of you. So I've organized a passenger for you.'

'A passenger?' said Corless.

'Yair.'

The woman in the taxi just ahead got out. It was Martha Rea. The driver hurried round to the back and began to lift cases from the boot.

'Oh, hell!' said Corless.

'Take it gently,' said Haig. 'I've been talking to Nightingale, and, as far as I can see, the only argument between you is what my fat aunt used to call dirty pride. I'll tell you something about Nightingale. That time she went back from Alchera Nine looking for you, I knew all about it. She asked me first if she could go.'

'So,' said Corless, 'all your ugliness with her was a gag.'

Haig nodded seriously. 'A matter of policy, Jock.'

Corless thought back to the conversation he had with Martha as she guided him to Alchera Nine. If Haig's attitude towards her had been a gag, then the greater part of her share of that conversation had been a gag, too. His face began to feel warm.

'Remember,' said Haig, 'pride has already been filed under Sins, Deadly, Cardinal. Dammit, why do you think she kept on wearing your perfume?'

Martha's lips were soft as she came towards the Goddess.

THE END

AFTERWORD

The Wakefield Crime Classics publication of *Ligny's Lake* last year introduced the work of a remarkable Australian crime fiction writer to a new generation of readers. S.H. Courtier (1909-74), though a Melbourne writer, had previously had only two of his novels published in Australia, *The Glass Spear* (1950), and *Gold for My Fair Lady* (1952), both by Invincible Press.

Though most of his work is no longer well known, Courtier was not an obscure figure in his own time, when he became, for instance, President of the Australian Centre of the International PEN Club. He was born at Kangaroo Flat, now a suburb of Bendigo, and both during his childhood and in later life moved around extensively, seeing a good portion of the continent. Since his father was a mine manager, he became well acquainted with the Australian gold country. He was educated at the University of Melbourne (Certificate of Education, first-class honours), so began his working life as a primary school teacher in rural Victoria and was later a principal in Melbourne schools for twelve years. He began writing, however, soon after he got married to Audrey Jennie George in 1932, and was able to publish serials, short stories and articles in both Australian and American magazines (including *Argosy*). He served for three years (1942-44) in the Australian Imperial Forces during World War Two and held the rank of Staff Sergeant. After the war, he lived in Highett, a Melbourne suburb, and later moved to Safety Beach, on Port Phillip Bay. He was handicapped by loss of speech following a stroke in 1967, but taught himself to speak again and wrote a further six novels before his death seven years later.

The variety of settings in Courtier's novels almost rivals that of Upfield. He likes to set his characters on the move, as can be seen in *Ligny's Lake* or in *Listen to the Mocking Bird* (1974), neither of which features a series hero. The Sydney detective, Ambrose Mahon, one of Courtier's two major detectives heroes, appeared in *The Glass Spear*, and he continued to serve well until 1964, although his other and more distinctive police detective, 'Digger' Haig, was by then well established. *Death in Dream Time* (1959) is, as far as we know, the second novel to feature Inspector Haig. Haig's first recorded case is *Now Seek My Bones* (1957), a thrilling murder mystery set in north Queensland, replete with crocodiles and crocodile men, snakes, buried treasure and black trackers. The 1959 novel is no less sensational and it, too, tests Haig's knowledge of Aboriginal lore.

Both Haig and Mahon are based in Sydney, although Courtier preferred to use up-country settings. The idea of an Aboriginal theme park located just north of the Queensland border with New South Wales seems bizarre, although so far as the fee-paying public can see of it, the dioramas are more tasteful and even artistic than is the case with the Bible lands of fiction, such as that in Peter Goldsworthy's *Honk If You Are Jesus* (1992). Carl Rusking, the artist, and Austin Flax, the former owner of a cattle station in Central Australia, have combined their talents to present, through nine Dioramas, 'the fundamental beliefs of the Aranda'. Rusking's account of the culture hero in the Dream Time, in the *Alchera* (an Aranda word more usually anglicised as the Alcheringa or Alchuringa – Upfield's preferred spelling) is dignified and solemn. It has been suggested by Philip Jones of the South Australian Museum that an analogy exists with the sculptor, William Ricketts, whose work (located principally at sites in the Dandenongs and Alice Springs) derives from close association with tribal Aborigines, and, although the comparison may not in general be helpful, the reference in chapter 4 to Apma raising his right arm and plucking 'sons, fully grown, from his armpit', does seem to recall Ricketts' work, as 'Rusking' is vaguely suggestive of the real sculptor's name, though his character is quite different. Considered merely as an artist, Rusking is genuine enough, and the reader agonises with him while Austin Flax is crudely vulgarising the commentary as Rusking is being questioned, particularly when it looks as if Flax is about to embark on the subject of infanticide. The procession through the dark forest (though it would be less confusing if it really were dark outside at the time), counterpointing the beauty of the timeless old dreaming storyline against the urgent police interrogation, is one of the novel's distinctive strengths.

It is characteristic of Courtier that clues should be, literally, cryptic. In *Death in Dream Time* the letter Corless receives from his cousin is used first obliquely, in order to associate the residents at Ungamillia with, as at first appears, various amounts of debt ('Julie Flax! £21.13.1d!'). Although the cipher gives Haig considerable trouble, which is not surprising in view of its use of a long and surprising Aboriginal phrase, the reader is apprised of its meaning at a relatively early stage of the narrative, so that its horrible implications will add terror to the plot.

Haig's reluctant explanation of the last three words in the cipher, '*atna-arilta-kuma*', is presented in a somewhat self-contradictory manner. He says first, 'It's one of the aspects of myall [wild black] life that is never mentioned. Not many people know about it, and just as well, too.' He then explains it as 'the rite for native girls corresponding to circumcision for youths. The initiates are deflowered with a stone knife, after which, as the textbooks say, the elders performing the ceremony enter into them'.

Editors of a text which, though not fully 'scholarly', is at least partly apologetic (to explain difficulties to the modern reader) and educative, are obliged to show whether what is being told here belongs to fact or fable. You begin by wondering which 'textbooks' Courtier had in mind, because the practice to which his detective refers seems not to be well known, even to anthropologists. In *The Golden Bough*, Frazer mentions the female equivalent of male sub-incisions occurring in Queensland, though his reference is to a tradition of disposing of the blood and so is not relevant to Courtier's novel. One standard textbook, *The Native Tribes of Central Australia*, by Baldwin Spencer and F.J. Gillen (1899, but available in a Dover Press reprint), describes *atna-arilta-kuma* but only as a ceremony performed on young women by older women. Perhaps Courtier received his information from conversations with Marie Reay, to whom homage is very likely paid (as Philip Jones, again, suggests) in the character of Martha Rea. Her book *Aborigines Now* was published in 1964.

Haig's account of *atna-arilta-kuma*, as becomes a great detective, is almost perfectly sound, as it happens, though a little garbled in transmission. It derives ultimately from C.F.T. Strehlow's monumental German text, *Die Aranda und Loritja: Stamme in Zentral-Australien* (1907), which has been translated but not published by Charles Chewings, as 'The Aranda and Loritja Tribes in Central Australia'. Rusking's first name, 'Carl', is probably given him in homage to Strehlow. As Strehlow describes it, the practice was one not of circumcision (though this may have been the effect in some cases) but of female sub-incision (Mallet refers to the male rite, which followed upon male circumcision, in chapter 7) and was called *parra-aralta-kama*. '*Parra*' and '*atna*' (sometimes '*alna*') denote the male and female parts, respectively; '*aralta*' refers to the ceremony (though Strehlow remarks that the female operation was not 'attached with any ceremonials or festivities'); '*kuma*' (Haig's '*kama*') means 'cut'. Three men acted in the performance of the ceremony and another anthropologist, W.E.

Roth (Roth is the authority cited by Frazer), notes that the actual operator was a 'very old man'. In the course of a few days, says Strehlow, this man 'goes to the maiden, lifts her up and cuddles her; then he commands her not to leave her future husband. He then cohabits with her; and in the following night the other two men, who assisted at the operation, by way of recompense for the services they rendered have fleshly intercourse with her also.' Between the operation and her marriage, the patient now has her place in the women's camp.

There is no serious indication that circumcision, let alone sub-incision, forms part of the initiation ceremonies the unsuspecting and credulous white females undergo when they are taken 'into the ground' for the thrill of meeting the *Iruntarinia* (Aranda spirit people). The point of the blackmail photographs is to threaten these 'initiates' with the revelation that during the ersatz rituals 'the elders performing the ceremony entered into them'. Very likely Courtier thought that without some really shocking background to the plot Laurie Moore would not have thought he was 'on to a filthy game. A game worse than murder'. When Haig refers to blackmail by means of the metaphor of bleeding ('We're not going to bleed them to death'), he may be punning on what goes on in the real ceremony, but whatever form of 'erotic magic' was being practised under the ground, it sickened so decent a man as Laurie Moore.

Throughout the novel, the tone used by the various characters in relation to the tribal beliefs and practices is indicative of their modern personalities and sensibilities. They do not measure the 'Alchera'; rather, the Alchera measures them, retaining its aloof mystery, its timeless distance from the relatively superficial contingencies of the Europeans. The gushing sentimentality of Mrs Ashwood, the romantic, hierophantic sentiment of Carl Rusking, the flippancy of Austin Flax, are not to be confused with the feelings of the author: to find those, we should probably prefer to take note of the 'mild, somewhat melancholy' manner of Inspector Haig. The crime of the *atna-arilta-kuma* does not reside in ceremonies of the past but in the villainous blackmailers of the present. None of us has to go far back, or even sideways, in our family trees to find cases of behaviour we find abhorrent. Our position is simply that no individuals are to be judged by what their ancestors did.

Deceit, found in all detective stories, is augmented in *Death in Dream Time* by the deployment of masks, an idea which is employed in various ways in Courtier's novels, not only through ciphers. The black face masks used by the villains directly reflect the idea of deception: appearances can never be trusted. The whole Dream Time display itself operates as a mask, seeming sacred, presented reverentially, but effectively a snare to draw in modern dreamers to what will end as nightmare. As Haig observes cynically (referring presumably only to Genghiz Khan), it is 'A stunt. But it gets 'em in.' The blasphemy of this appropriation of what is secret, almost taboo, is not the author's blasphemy: he is the one who exposes it, who brings it to light. The mask more subtly might be of the man above suspicion, the man in the police uniform, innocently in love, as it appears. It might belong to the sympathetic woman. Ironically, the wearers of masks can be induced to unmask only when the 'straight' people begin to put on masks the enemies of the law have provided for them. The good Sergeant Clough puts on a mask and becomes a dummy or lay figure. As he launches at the critical moment into his explanation (meant to draw Constable Bailey down into the trap at the bottom of the tree – the tree which is the most cunning mask of all), Haig pauses, and 'his dark face thinned into a hard mask'.

Haig is an exceptionally ugly man. In his case, ugliness is a mask for honesty and a great capacity for friendship. It is not for nothing that he is called 'Digger' by his friends, and that he says of himself, 'I dig the facts out.' Digging is also in this story being undertaken by Austin Flax, but Austin digs in the wrong place, which is probably just as well for him. Digger

Haig not only digs for the facts, but also files them. Like the Aranda with their Dream Time Alchera, what Haig is basically filing in his explanation is what he says others should do: 'File it under the way things happen.'

It is because of the weakness of their planning, the way they do not allow for 'the way things happen', that the conspirators lose: they confuse dreaming with reality.

MICHAEL J. TOLLEY AND PETER MOSS

WAKEFIELD CRIME CLASSICS

Peter Moss and Michael J. Tolley, general editors of the Wakefield Crime Classics series, are colleagues at the University of Adelaide. Late in 1988, they began assembling a series of Australian 'classic' crime fiction and soon realised that the problem was not going to be one of finding sufficient works of high quality, but of finding a bold enough publisher fired with the same vision.

This series revives forgotten or neglected gems of crime and mystery fiction by Australian authors. Many of the writers have established international reputations but are little known in Australia. In the wake of the excitement generated by the new wave of Australian crime fiction writers, we hope that the achievements of earlier days can be justly celebrated.

If you wish to be informed about new books as they are released in the Wakefield Crime Classics series, send your name and address to Wakefield Press, Box 2266, Kent Town, South Australia 5071, phone (08) 362 8800, fax (08) 362 7592.

Also available in

WAKEFIELD CRIME CLASSICS

LIGNY'S LAKE
by S.H. Courtier

A dead man alive at Melbourne's Festival Hall . . . a merino-shaped lake . . . a stolen copy of Thoreau's *Walden* . . . ASIO's wall of silence.

Sandy Carmichael can pick up the jigsaw pieces, but to fit them together, he needs to risk his life.

Ligny's Lake is a puzzling story of suspense that weirdly echoes the disappearance of Prime Minister Harold Holt.

'S.H. Courtier is unjustly neglected. His works show a good narrative style, ingenious plots, and integral settings that are powerfully atmospheric.'
Whodunit?

'An intriguing and ingenious novel'
Stan Barney, *Canberra Times*